I0788579

Stella's Revenge

Stella's Revenge

Patricia Brothers

Copyright

The Butterfly Typeface Publishing
PO BOX 56193
Little Rock Arkansas 72215

Dedication

As always, all the things I do – it is for you two: Aaliyah and Torrie, my perfect Dynamic Duo! Remember, if it were easy, everyone would be doing it.
Reach for the stars. You are already stars in my book; I love you two so much!

Mommy and Sissies, you know that I heart you guys so much! Thank you so much for believing in my dreams.

Honorable Mentions:
Keyuana & Harmonie
Darron II, Dominic (DJ & Desi)
Dontay
Kourtney
Aniyah & ArRell

Family is everything, and I love each and every one of you.

Also by Patricia Brothers

Death by Imagination

Table of Contents

Foreword

The story of Stella is purely derived from the actions of misbehaved kids. We have all heard stories. You may even see someone you know (or know of) doing some of the same actions in the book.

As you read the story, try to see it from her eyes, not as who we are or who we have become as adults. Also, we know all too well how children are sexualized and overly sexual at young ages. Stella is no exception. While you may become uncomfortable with certain situations, ask yourself why? Why do you feel uncomfortable? Why is she so vulnerable to behave in such a way?

Another thing I want to stress to you, the reader, is the liberties I take as the author. Knocking down that "fourth wall" is something I enjoy. It is my way of holding your hand and giving you a guided tour of the story.

Forgive the authorial intrusion and have fun with the story! We all have intrusive thoughts; we just know not to act upon them.

And although this features a child – this is NOT a children's book.

Patricia Brothers

Acknowledgments

Iris Williams, you are truly an inspiration, and I thank you for being there and helping me to achieve my dreams. Without you, none of this would be possible. Your guidance is appreciated through this journey. I truly could not have done this without you. Thank you.

To my fans and supporters, you guys are everything to me! Thank you so much for being there and enjoying the ride with me!

You ever hated life so much? You ever feel like your world fell apart and you felt so helpless? At first, it felt like there was nothing you could do to fix it. Then you become so angry and everything starts to bubble over? Then no matter how much you try to fix it, it just gets worse? Then a calm comes over you and you just roll with it. You just hold on, looking for your happy ending.

I do not know if I will get there. But I can tell you this; I am about to take you on a hell of a ride that is my life. Strap in because the shit you are about to read is definitely not what I expected my life to be. Well, not all of it anyway. If you are going to be judgmental, just stop right here.

If you want to know why I am the way that I am - keep going. There is lots of tea (or you can brew your own). By the time I am done, you will probably want a drink.

Either way, this is my story.

Prelude

I sat there, looking at Molly, and all I wanted to do was stab her in the eyes.

Molly was this pretty, little perfect angel. Everyone just *loved* her. She had blonde hair and blue-grey eyes. Even her smile was perfect. ALL the teachers liked her.

But I knew she was far from an angel. She was a stuck-up bitch who knew how to play the role well.

It's not that I'm jealous of her. I just HATE her!

Oh well. It seems lately that I hate *everybody*.

Except for my mom. I love my mom more than anyone else in the world. Or anything for that matter.

Moving on.

We were sitting in class and Little Miss Perfect just *had* to bring up Christmas. (Insert eye roll.) How old are we?

She raised her hand and out came, "Ms. Huffman? We have a little time to kill before break starts. Wouldn't it be a great idea to talk about our Christmas plans? I mean. If it doesn't offend anyone." She looked back at me.

Did I mention how much I hate her?

Ms. Huffman grasped at her heart and smiled. I guess Molly's request would melt any adult's heart since, as kids get older, they really don't talk about this stuff anymore.

shrug As if I really give a damn.

I couldn't help but roll my eyes. (For real this time.) Ms. Huffman caught me, but she must've not paid it any mind because she kept it moving. Good for her. I do kinda like her, and I'd hate for her to get in the way. Though, in a sense, it really didn't matter to me if she did.

Now, to the hilarious part.

So, we were sitting there talking about world peace, Santa, Christ, traveling plans, and all the other crap that comes with Christmas.

Then, Ms. Huffman started asking us individually what we wanted for Christmas. After the speech made by Little Miss Perfect, how could any of us top that?

Oh. I have an idea. An awful idea. A wonderful, *awful* idea. (Please keep up with the Pop Culture this important.) I smiled. And on cue, I was next …

"So, Stella," Ms. Huffman smiled with that I-love-my-classroom teacher smile that teachers have, "what would you like for Christmas?"

In my head, I thought of a million 'sweet' things to say, but what came out was nothing sweeter than pure gold.

I sat up very prim and proper. (I even batted my eyes.) I put on my sweetest smile and said, "I would like for all of you to die, starting with… her."

If you didn't guess, I was pointing at Molly.

The 'Oh my god' gasps in the room were loud. Ms. Huffman nearly fainted. And Molly? She threw up all over her brand-new dress.

I sat back, locked my hands behind my head, crossed my legs and smiled the widest smile I could muster.

Did I mention that Molly's worst fear was dying? No? Oh. #SorryNotSorry

The mention of her name and death in the same sentence always caused the worst reactions. Once, she even passed out!

This is because her grandfather died horribly right before her eyes.

I wish I could have seen that. Secretly, she may have been the cause of his passing and now she feels guilty.

Ordinarily, under different circumstances, I probably would have been a bit more understanding. But things are different now.

I'll tell you about my transformation later.

First, I was still reveling in the look of horror on Molly's face. The class and Ms. Huffman were an added bonus. Molly was supposed to have been the only intended target.

If I knew I could cause her pain and strife without being labeled a bully… I truly would. Image mattered to me, but only because it was better to do bad things when people didn't expect you to.

Revenge was sweet.

Secret revenge was even sweeter.

Chapter One

That Damn Cat

 It's taking everything in me right now not to end this quickly. But I like what I'm doing. Not only is it giving me time to study, but it's also preparing me for my next victim.

The cat lay there gasping its last breath. The meows are barely audible. Thank God. Boy oh boy, would I be in trouble if they knew what I was doing.

This cat has evaded me for soooooo long!

Again, there is the faint sound of the cat's "meeoow."

I used to think this cat was like a roaring lion. The way it pranced around our home like it thought it was Queen Sheba or somebody. I mean, Karen would come running as soon as she heard it purr!

It's just a stupid cat, for Pete's sake.

But oh, no. Not according to Karen. I know Karen likes this cat more than she likes me, but she is good at putting on faces like Molly. Something like this was bound to happen.

So, here is Karen's precious cat tied (more like stapled) to this 8X8 piece of board. It's fabulous. I did it exactly how I learned in biology. The only difference is those cats were dead. This one will be too, but not yet.

I took a little more time to stretch her out just a bit more. That had to hurt. I wanted it to. Not my problem, though. Queen Sheba had the unfortunate luck of being Karen's cat.

What's so bad about Karen? Let me tell you. Here comes a little of the back story.

My mom and dad (Should I even call him that?) were married long before I was born. Ms. Johnson, my dad's old secretary (I mean REALLY OLD), was the best. She always gave me candy when my parents weren't looking. Things were perfect.

Ms. Johnson finally retired, and that's when the trouble began.

My dad hired Karen. Now, Karen had all the same perks as Ms. Johnson. I didn't think that was right or fair. Why did she have to come to our house *all the time?* I mean, really?! She couldn't be that great at her job if she had to constantly consult my dad. But according to my dad, she was "fabulous."

right *She gave me a headache!*

One thing led to another and the next thing I know, me and Mom are about to have nervous breakdowns. We were leaving my dad and our luxury home!

Not to say that our new two-bedroom condo is bad. As a matter of fact, I like it there. I made friends. I love my school.

EVERYTHING.

But then here comes the lovely Karen Johnson, AKA, KJ. She disrupts things even further by insisting that my dad should get full custody of me because being without me is stressing him out. I'm sure she is the one being stressed since it's her job to transport me between my parents. I wasn't even giving her trouble … yet.

Karen knew that my dad would win the custody case that he quickly filed in the middle of the divorce. Really? That was all worked out before her "suggestions." He was well connected, had the better lawyer friends, and then you add Mom's mental state. Nor could she afford the additional costs for another lawyer or services.

Can you blame her? She's losing her home, lover, and life as she knows it.

Mom being on antidepressants and seeing a therapist didn't help her case.

labeled #unfit

But she isn't/wasn't. Mom comes to get me every chance she gets. I am not an inconvenience to *her*.

My dad, however, is a different story. Since this new Karen came into the picture, everything about me is an inconvenience.

I can't tell you how many plays, dance, or orchestra recitals he's missed. I play four instruments, but I don't think my dad has ever heard me play one.

Why didn't it ever occur to him that I needed him too?

Karen attends my events, but only to piss off my mom. I heard her tell my dad that she would support me through this tough transition and felt the arts were a good outlet for me.

I call bull.

And to think, I wasn't even bad then.

So, THAT'S what's so bad about Karen so far. At least to start.

I consider this payback for making my life a living hell.

OH, and WTF is up with this health food, organic shit that Karen and my dad insist on forcing on me? Another reason I absolutely hate her.

Now, my mom, she's a different story. You would swear she's like half black because *her* food is awesome.

No bias. Really.

Mom does have a lot of black friends. They put her cooking skills on point. Mom's food is good, and whatever pointers or help she got from her friends, she took our food to the next level.

LOL *I learned quickly what having 'the -itis' after eating meant!*

Before the divorce, the one thing I always looked forward to was the holidays. We ALWAYS had tons of friends over and plenty of food. But then it changed because one of her close friends became religious, so Mom hosted 'just because' get-togethers so that her friend didn't feel excluded.

That's the kind of woman my mom is. She cares about everyone. I love that about her. And everyone loves my mom.

The first Christmas I spent with *that man* after he was awarded custody was hard. I asked him to invite my mom and friends over and his response was, "Well, honey. I don't think that's a good idea. You know your stepmother will be here too and that wouldn't be fair to her."

I could have punched him in the throat!

Oh, but boy, did he regret that decision! LMAO!

"Meeeee...." The cat's cries interrupted my thoughts.

Oh, shit the cat is dying. Jesus!

I am not ready for Queen Sheba to die. As I jab the huge needle into her, I wonder if I'd make a good nurse.

This needle is effing HUGE.

I'm not gentle. It's just not my style.

Actually, there was a time when I could have been a good nurse, but they (that man and Karen) have changed me.

Once upon a time, I really did want to be a nurse and help those who couldn't help themselves. But that all changed when that man married Karen.

I mean honestly, I hope you see where this is going, right? I know two wrongs don't make it right. But sometimes you just do what you gotta do. You know? It wasn't my desire. She just messed things up from the beginning.

I mean honestly this woman had the same first name as your wife. Same last name as your secretary and office manager. To me, you're just trying to rekindle some old memory that you once had.

Chapter Two

Why the Cat Had to Go

Queen Sheba (as I began to refer to her) wasn't always my enemy.

I tried to play nice. I tried to be the good girl. And at the time I *was* the good girl. I even let the stupid thing sleep in *my* bed. I'd pet it. I'd brush it. Gave it treats. You know, all things you do to care for pets.

Three years ago, I had just turned 10. I was sitting on the floor watching cartoons eating a bowl of Neapolitan ice cream. I went to caress her, and the damn bitch scratched me!

I knew at that moment I would get revenge. It was inevitable.

Cats are smart. I'm sure she noticed the change in my attitude towards her. She avoided me at all costs and was successful, until now. And that was okay. The time it took to catch her gave me more than enough time to contemplate exactly what I was going to do and how I was going to do it.

So, with enough treats and some coercion, I trapped Queen Sheba and quickly went to the crawl space where I had already stashed everything I needed.

I chose this place because it was my own private discovery. My parents had no idea it was here. They will never know what happened here or find Queen Sheba's body. Unless I tell them. Or the smell becomes noticeable upstairs.

*Oh, and those treats? They were laced with morphine that I stole a long time ago from his office. *LMAO**

As the cat lay there, the first thing I did was tape its mouth just enough for it to be muffled but loud enough for me to be able to hear her screams.

And there's a lot of that.

Next, I slit her open from stem to sternum being careful not to hit any organs or risk a premature bleed out.

I give myself a once-over (can't risk getting blood all over my clothes) and laugh as I thought, *I must look like a friggin' doctor from the CDC or something.*

As I listen to the cat moan, I ponder over what to do next. *Shall I pull out the whiskers? Where are the wire pliers? Oh. Right here.*

My leg had covered them up. As I lean over to get the pliers, I looked Queen Sheba dead in her eyes. Animals are not dumb. She reads all the hate in my face. And her moans grow louder.

I pull one whisker out and then another. One by one until there are none left.

And yes, yes, I am torturing her.

The sounds she makes sound like the cat was *actually* crying. I'd like to think so anyway.

Ha. Ha. Ha. Haaaaaaaa!

I reach over for the brand new, very sharp pair of scissors Karen recently purchased for her sewing and knitting and crap.

Yes. Yes, I decide. *I will slowly cut off her ears.*

I start, and there's the blood. It trickles into a little puddle on the floor. I wait about 2 seconds or so between each snip. This way the Queen here has enough time to get over the initial cut before I make the next one.

So, it goes like this: snip, meow, wait, snip, meow, wait…

It takes about 5-10 minutes just to cut off one ear. I want her to know just how much I hate her.

This is so weird, wrong, and fun.

Welp. That ear is gone. I take the glue gun and glue it to the wall. The poor thing's eyes follow me as I do it.

Man, this is gross! On to ear number two!

I laugh as I consider asking Queen Sheba, "Can you hear me now?"

Oh crap. I forgot about the boiling hot water.

I get the water and release a few drops in her eyes from the turkey baster. The first drop sends the cat into a got damn frenzy!

That's gotta hurt! Damn!

"Bet ya kinda wish you never scratched me now huh?" I whisper into her ear hole as I wonder if she can hear me.

"Stella!" Karen's voice startles me.

"Stella!"

I knew this damn cat wouldn't last through dinner.

Oh well. Time to end it.

I pick up dad's brand-new scalpel. As I look at my reflection in the shiny blade, I think, "You really are a bad person."

Smile

With precision, I plunge the scalpel deep into the cat's heart and down she goes!

I shed off all the medical gear I was wearing. Careful not to get any of the cat's blood on me. I gather the scalpel, scissors, and pliers and put them in a Ziploc bag. I'd stolen what I needed from my dad's job. I'm smart. I knew not to leave evidence that could be traced back to me.

Now that the cat has met her demise, it's time for Karen to do the same.

This Karen is the one responsible for my dad leaving my mom and for me being taken away.

Ugh! How dare you marry a woman with the same name as my mother!

This Karen has no idea what's about to happen to her. She should have never taken my daddy (once upon a time, he was my daddy) away. She should have never tried to do this whole "family" thing.

I didn't like her from the moment I saw her. She pretended to be an assistant or intern of sorts, but what I saw was a young woman in seductive clothing leaning in too close to my dad.

I see you, Karen. You are not fit to take my mother's place. You're only doing this to stay close to my dad and his money.

But that's okay.

Your vows did say, "Until death do us part."

And well, it's time for you to part.

Chapter Three

The Fake Karen

I'm a child prodigy. I know just as much as any chemist.

At the age of six, I was convinced that I wanted to be a doctor, just like my father. I read his medical books and studied the terminology. At this point, I know more about the latest drugs and medical advances than he does. At times, he even relies on me to keep him abreast of updated material in the medical world.

Father. What a strange word.

That man thinks he is a good *father* or *dad,* but it's all for show. A good father, dad, or man, for that matter, would never split up his family. He would never leave his wife. He would never cheat on her. And he definitely would never choose another woman over his child. No. He's not a good anything.

He lied. His vows meant nothing. He should die too, or at least suffer. It's his fault that he can't be a real man.

Revenge. That's all that matters now.

"Stella." Oh, how I wish this bitch would just shut the fuck up!

It's clear Karen isn't going to give up calling me, so I leave the crawl space and the dead cat. I'll come back later to finish clearing up the evidence. Right now, shutting her up is more important.

I quickly looked at my reflection in the mirror — not a single drop of blood on me.

Perfect. Nothing out of place.

"Yes ma'am," I say and surprise myself with how sweet I sound.

"Honey, it's time to eat," Karen says just as sweetly, "I made your favorite: chicken with mac and cheese."

"Mmm," I mumble, "I can't wait."

I hate mac and cheese. Well, her mac and cheese, anyway.

Karen walks over to hug me. I want to grab a fork and stab her. Her perfume reeks. It doesn't smell like it does on my mom.

Why would he buy that for her? Same name. Same scent. Makes no sense!

That shows you that a part of him is holding on to my mom. That was always Mom's favorite perfume.

Never mind, Stella, I think as I struggle to hold in a grimace. *Get through dinner and be done with it.*

"It smells great Kar–I mean, Mom."

She makes me call her that, and that asshole enforces it.

"I worked really hard," Karen beams. "I know how great you've been doing in school and wanted to give you a special treat from the healthy stuff we usually eat."

"Yes! Finally," I say, but don't really mean it. I know I convinced Karen that she's the best mom ever. I need to continue to play the role.

I can't wait for the moment when *this* Karen **CEASES to EXIST**. Tuh. Huh!

Dinner went, let's say well enough for them not to suspect anything is wrong. But then ...

"Has anyone seen Passion?" Karen asks, deeply concerned. "I haven't seen her all day."

Holy shit!

My heart drops. She looked genuinely hurt. I wasn't expecting to care. Now, do I lose my shit and confess? Or do I laugh because *I Know What I Did This Winter*?

I laugh inside at the irony. I so hope you caught that, right? No? Go ask a friend and then come back to me.

"Nope. Can't say that I have," I say, faking concern.

"Well, honey. You know, cats sometimes just like to be left alone," He says.

If you can see how hard I roll my eyes.

"I know. But when I went to put out cat treats, I thought they smelled funny," Karen continues.

I perk up. "Did you taste them?"

"No, silly girl."

"Oh," I said, disappointed. But then, "Not being funny, but maybe you should? What if they made her sick?"

"That would mean I would get sick too, crazy child!"

No shit.

"Then you could sue," I pursue.

"The only problem is, I wouldn't get anything for me," Karen mused. "The cat maybe, but even then that wouldn't be much."

"Oh," I say and go back to eating this dry-ass food.

"Maybe Love," he grabs her hand, "when we go for our walk, we can see if she somehow escaped the house."

At this moment, I fight the urge to go to the crawl space and bring out the dead cat.

"Yeah, maybe," Karen smiles. "Babe, what would I do without you?"

I just threw up. Aren't they a little too old for this shit?

No really, vomit is spewing everywhere.

This shit is so fucking awful. I get up from the table and leave them to clean it up.

I go upstairs to shower.

Afterward, I sneak out the house (as usual) and head over to Tara's. Hopefully, her brother is home. He's 16, and I have a crush on him.

I'm almost 14, so no big deal, right?

I get to Tara's, and no one is home. Dang. I guess I should have called first.

It's ok; the time alone gave me time to think about how to get my revenge on this Karen. She's so predictable.

It's going to be fun and easy!

Chapter Four

How I Started

 The next day I wake up before everyone. I slip into the kitchen to put the crushed pills I took from my dad's medical bag into the coffee creamer.

I figure if Karen's blood was ever checked, they'd conclude that she was using drugs, or my dad was drugging her. I honestly don't care either way, as long as my hands are clean. Besides, considering how holistic Karen is, I seriously doubt they will draw blood anyway.

After that, I lace the orange juice with Dilaudid. LOTS of it.

No one drinks it but Karen anyway.

Drugging her isn't as much fun as trapping the cat, but the slow process just may make it worthwhile. I mean, it's only fair since she slowly stole my dad.

I crept back into bed and waited for Mr. and Mrs. Clockwork to rise.

As I lay in bed, the coffee aroma begins to fill the air, and I know they'll be up soon.

Oh, the sweet smell of revenge!

Karen walks through the house opening curtains and blinds to let the sunshine through.

She really isn't as nice as she seems. After all, she intentionally split up the family. She has got to go.

The smell of sex and my mom's perfume arrives in my room before she does. I don't think that's how it's supposed to go. I guess she didn't bathe after.

Yes, I know about sex. I know a lot of other things too. I MIGHT get to that a little later. Might.

"Stella," Karen says in that sing-song, high pitched, "I just got my brains fucked out of me; life is wonderful" voice. "Wake up, Darling."

She opens the curtains and smiles back at me. She is so annoying. What does he see in her?

"She's just like Mom," he once said to me.

Really? There is absolutely no way this woman is "just like Mom!"

Her death will be sweet. It has to be precise. It has to be timed just right. Because in a few months school will be out and I will be reunited with *my* Karen, *my* mom. The Karen who carried me for nine months. The Karen who suffered birth pangs to give birth to her angel, the only child to survive after three miscarriages.

THAT KAREN is MY mom.

I wait for her to leave the room and then dress quickly so I can revel in my work. I want to watch Karen and David (that man who used to be my dad) partake in an unknown attempt to end their lives.

I watch carefully as Karen pours a glass of orange juice for herself and makes two cups of coffee, generously adding cream and handing one to her husband.

I nearly choke on my toast in excitement.

"Are you okay?" David asks.

"Mm-hmm. Of course," I respond, clearing my throat. "It just went down the wrong way."

"Here, have some juice, baby," Karen offers and extends her cup to me.

As if I would EVER drink after her!

"Um, no thanks," I politely decline. "I'll just get some water."

Holy crap! That was close.

David accepts Karen's generosity and drinks some of her orange juice.

Sweet!

I look at them in the most loving way, willing them to finish the juice and coffee.

Maybe I should have tested it to be sure there was enough in it. Uhhhh, on second thought, nope. My blood has to be clean, just in case. But then again, if it's not in my system... Oh, stop it.

I'm becoming paranoid.

Chapter Five

She's Really Sick and He's Exhausted

 Two weeks have gone by, and Karen is getting sicker by the day. Because of her religious views, she refuses to see a doctor, even my dad. This makes things even easier for me.

This is golden!

I can hear Karen praying incessantly. Every day. Today, her praying is infuriating. Irritated, I close my bedroom door and turn the music up.

David (no point calling him Dad anymore) has been picking up extra shifts at the hospital to make ends meet since Karen hasn't been working.

It's amazing how things went so haywire in such a short period of time.

To play the role of caring child, I pretend to be concerned and offer to be Karen's caregiver. And *that* leaves me alone with her CONSTANTLY.

My plan is going perfectly. I couldn't have planned it better if I wanted to.

Despite Karen's moaning (she reminds me of Queen Sheba) and praying, I manage to finish my homework and take a nap.

When I wake up, I decide it's time to feed Karen. On today's menu: Soup Du Jour AKA: rat poison.

Oh, come on. Don't look like that. It's not gonna kill her. Well, maybe not today. (If only) And it's not like I put rat droppings in it. Or did I?

We live in a luxury home, they drive expensive cars, and I attend one of the most prestigious schools. So why are there areas of our home that aren't so clean?

I guess Karen had other more important things on her mind than making sure we don't have rats! I can definitely say we didn't when Mom was here. Well, she was too busy spending all of the money, apparently, and hiding it.

David comes pouring in really late tonight. You can practically hear the exhaustion. I walk down the stairs and just stare at him. He looks so frail, sitting in the big poppa chair.

I mean, God, dude! Eat a cheeseburger, at least.

With all that has been going on, he hasn't been working out or eating right at all.

I'm not sympathetic. Just giving you a visual.

So, his once sought-after physique is quickly becoming a bag of bones, and it's only been a couple of weeks!

Five minutes has gone by and he never looks up or notices me. Well, I guess it's no different than when he wasn't busy, and in love with that tramp.

I turn to go back up the stairs; then I hear something faint.

Oh no. I know he's not. Oh yes, he is!

I almost want to jump up and down! He's effing crying!

Dang it! Oh, this is priceless. I hope the camera that I hid is getting all of this.

I sit crisscross on the floor and just swoon back forth like my favorite jam is on.

Oh, poor David. Do you know that my mom went through these same emotions?

Only I held her. I uplifted her. I did her make-up. I dressed her. I forced her to live when she wanted to end it all.

Are you there yet? Are you ready to end your life?

One thing's for sure, two things for certain, I thought, *I ain't gonna do any of that for you. You brought this on yourself. Get on somewhere with that.*

Ain't nobody got time for that.

See what I did there? No? You really need to learn Pop Culture.

BUT I will pretend. Just enough to keep the police off me.

Why should Karen suffer alone? David is just as much to blame. Oh, I got this!

I walk up to him with the saddest face I can muster.

"Oh, Daddy." (*I have to on GP.*) "It's gonna be okay." I guess I startled him.

He grabs my hand and says, "I know, Pumpkin. I just wish she would go to a doctor, let a doctor come here, or, hell, let *me* check her out."

In the back of my head, I'm like, *hell no!*

I rub David's back and lay my head on his shoulder.

Speaking of a cheeseburger, let me feed him. That's what good daughters do, right?

"Dad, you look so frail," I say with concern. "Let me get you something to eat. I have a surprise for you."

What?! I do have a surprise for him. I'm not always mean. Well...

"Now here's the thing, Daddy," I warn him. "You can't ask me any questions in any shape, form, or fashion. Just know that I got it, perfectly legal. I know how much you used to enjoy it and maybe still secretly enjoy it. Ok? I'm telling you. You are going to love the surprise I have for you."

David has absolutely nothing to say. Perfect. He looks at me with these "she's so wonderful" eyes and nods his head in agreement. I stare back, looking through him. He's been dead to me for a long time now.

I head to the kitchen to fix him something to eat.

Since Karen hasn't been in the kitchen, I have been tasked (I tasked myself) with preparing anything edible around this joint.

I created a little space for my 'secret' goodies.

So, what 'secret' goody is on today's menu for dear old Dad? Hmmm. Oh, the spaghetti!

Never mind it's only a little over a week old, and I saw mold growing on it. Mold is healthy, right? I mean, that's how they make penicillin and blue cheese. So, there is that.

I laughed as I thought, *I could really be on some cooking show. I'd call it Poison Control: Food So Good You Die.*

I pull out the spaghetti. I also pull out my jar of *special sauce* AKA: Karen's menstrual blood. I bang a couple of dishes together to make it sound good. I mix the blood in the sauce before I warm it up.

Yes. I have on gloves. That's disgusting.

Next, I pull out the beer that I convinced my neighbor to buy because I wanted to surprise David (since he's been working so hard). I heat up the chicken that I fried too. The vegetables are spoiled a bit, but after warming them up, I added a little seasoning and butter and voila! A meal fit for a king who's about to lose his throne.

When I take David his plate, I notice that miraculously he was able to shed his clothes. I give him a cloth to wipe his hands while I set up the tray table.

"Mmm," David inhales. "Baby. I forgot you know how to cook," he exclaims as I set the food down on the tray in front of him.

"Well, eat up then, Dad," I say cheerily. "You've been working so hard. You deserve a break today. Oh! Wait!"

I dash back into the kitchen, open the beer and another jar I have stashed. This one has some of Queen Sheba's urine. (I emptied her bladder before I killed her.)

It had been challenging to keep the stench from smelling up the place. I had to buy so many air fresheners!

I take a dropper (can't spill any) and add it to the beer.

David has been drinking the coffee creamer, so this is nothing right? Besides, he still hadn't gotten sick yet.

Don't judge me.

I kind of skip back into the living room and *Nightmare on Elm Street* is on, but that's not what stops me in my tracks! David is DE-VOUR-ING the food!

My God! Can my night get any better?!

I set the beer down, and he looks. He cocks his head to the right like a dog trying to understand what his master is saying. I throw up my hands and smirk.

"Surprise!" I shout and hand him the bottle.

"Oh right," he finally says. "I can't ask how."

And just like that, he downs about half the bottle.

Do you know how hard it is to hold my composure right now?

"That's right," I say and take the remote and turn up the volume on the TV. Not because I want to watch this stupid crap, but to keep him distracted.

Faintly, I hear Karen calling. I glance back at the stairs.

Those bed sores must be really hurting.

"So, how was work?"

"It was, well, work. Lots of stuff going on today from broken bones to gunshot wounds."

"Anything new in the medical world?"

"Oh, babes. We haven't had these talks in a long time huh?"

"No." I nod towards the food, "Eat up." I eye the food as if I can will it down his throat.

"You know the medical field. Ever changing."

smirk *Yeah dude I know, but do you?*

"Why don't you come hang with me tomorrow?"

"Who will take care of Kar-, I mean, mom?"

"Jesus. What was I thinking? I've put so much on you."

"It's ok," I quickly recover. "I'm here for everyone."

"Yeah, but who's here for you?"

"I think I'm a pretty big girl."

"That you are, my dear. That you are." David gives up much too easily. "Have you talked to your mom?"

"Which one?" I smirk, and he erupts in laughter. I haven't heard that in a while.

"Yeah. You got me there."

"I know you were referring to my biological mother," I say and laugh with him. "I just wanted to hear you laugh."

NOT.

"But yes," I continue. "I talk to her every day. It gets kinda lonely around here ya' know?"

"Yes, I do, Sweet Pea. Yes, I do. I gotta fix that."

Oh shit! No DON'T fix it! Damn it! I laid it on a little too much. Switch subjects.

On TV, Freddy just got another victim. Although it's hella funny, I play scared and jump.

"Ooo, dad," I say. "How did we used to watch this stuff?"

With a mouthful of food, he looks up and says, "I guess it is pretty gruesome huh?" Then takes another swig of beer.

Sweet Jesus! This is great.

We sit there and finish watching the movie. It is well past midnight.

David passes out on the couch. He looks uncomfortable. I just leave him there.

I won't even bother to wake him. Hope he oversleeps and has bad body aches.

I walk off and don't look back.

Chapter Six

Wishes and Disappointments

The next morning, I get my wish.

 David oversleeps, and I sit in the big poppa chair, watching him the entire time.

His phone is vibrating like crazy! I continue to watch. When he begins to stir, I hightail it to my room.

It's been about 12 hours or so since I checked on *the thing*. She's out of it, and I'm sure she may not remember.

Finally, he's wide awake, and I can hear the screaming from my room.

"I'm late! My whole body hurts! Where's my phone? I've got to call in and let them know I overslept."

I smile as I hear him fumbling around while he listens to whomever is on the phone trying to brief him on what is going on in the office during his absence.

Finally, I hear David run up the steps and into the bathroom.

Oh, the groans. It's like music to my ears.

He is so preoccupied with his own issues; he doesn't even think to check on her.

This couldn't have gone any better.

I leave my room, prepared to go to school. Just as I step out of my room, I see him dash down the hall. He stops short, and the look in his eyes had me shook for a second. I play it cool.

"Hey Dad," I say absently. "I thought you were gone."

"No. I overslept," he says frantically. "Maybe I should stay home. I need a break."

"Well, you know that we are already having trouble keeping up with the bills," I say, feigning diplomacy. "And it's only been a few weeks."

"This is true," David says quickly. "But I'm thinking of you at the moment."

No, don't. Really.

"Dad. Really. I'm ok." (Plus, I don't need you to see what I am doing.)

"Yeah. But I want us to skip like we used to do before all of this. I want to go to the parlor for ice cream. I want to take you to the movies and lunch. I just want to *chill*." (He sighs.)

The sound in his voice gets to me and makes me want to just break down and give in.

"Ok. Dad. Let's do it."

Then he reminds me of why I'm doing this in the first place.

"I wonder if your mom is available to watch Karen," he somehow fixes his mouth to ask.

In my head, I stab him in the left eye about five times.

Did he really just say that? I know that those words DID NOT just come out of his mouth. Are you so daring to ask your ex-wife to watch over the woman you left her for? Did that even remotely make sense?

My blood runs hot as fire, and I swear that Satan is doing a dance in my eyes. I coolly return back to this world.

"You know. That is a very good idea," I say instead. "She would be in safe hands."

"You're right, Pumpkin," he says, hopeful.
"I'm going to call your mother, change, and I'll be right out."

"Ok," I say, but I was looking forward to Mom telling him what he could do with his wife.

David walks into the bedroom and leaves the door half-open, so I hear him speaking to Mom. She's on speaker as he changes.

 "Hey, Karen. It's David."

"I know. Hey."

"Um. Listen. Stella isn't going to school today because I'm going to spend some quality time with her."

"Oh, that's wonderful. I know she's going to love that."

She's so roses and rainbows.

"Yeah. That's kind of why I am calling. I need a favor."

"Oh, really?"

Score one for Mom on the sarcasm.

"Yeah. Listen. I know you're off today and it would mean so much to me if…"

"You really want me to go?"

"Uh. No," David says cautiously. "You know Karen is not doing well."

"Yes," Mom says with attitude. "What does that have to do with me?"

Get it, Mom!

"Well, I'm hoping you could stay with her while we're out. I really want to do this with Stella. Can you at least do this?"

(Insert hesitation.) "Only because of Stella am I willing to do this."

And just like that, my bubble bursts.

Damn Mom! Like WTF?!?!

"Great. I'm going to shower and get dressed. So, be here in an hour?"

"Yeah."

The call disconnects, and before David can even get out of the bedroom door, I am downstairs and out the door.

I never walked so fast to get to the bus stop.

Luckily, the bus is early.

Chapter Seven

Fun with Molly

 I get on the bus and walk to the back. I must have had some kind of look on my face because no one even bothers to say hello until …

"Hi, Stella!"

TF? Why is she speaking to me? Why is she even at the back of the bus?

"Hey."

"You know. I've been thinking. Why don't we bury the hatchet and start over?" She extends her hand as if I would be willing to shake it.

"Number one," I begin. "Who in the hell says, 'bury the hatchet?' Number two, I DON'T LIKE YOU. There is nothing on this earth that I would love more than for you to DIE right now. LEAVE ME THE HELL ALONE!!"

Molly immediately throws up in her hands.

Nice. I should scream die over and over.

At that moment, the ENTIRE bus erupts into a fury of comments:

"Dang, Stella."

"Killer dude."

"She a muthaduckin' gangsta."

"Welcome to the dark side!"

"Hold up – white girl getting crazy. Let me off this bus before she starts shooting."

"Don't hurt'em, Big Dawg."

Molly begins crying. Good. That leads me to believe all those other kids feel the same way I do.

Bet she won't try that shit again.

After that, the bus gets very quiet. Everyone is either looking at their phone, a book, or whatever. So, I decided to be productive and use the time to apply super glue to Molly's hair.

That was the best 30 minutes of my life. So far.

No one is even paying attention to me. Once the bottle is empty, I throw it out of the window. Nobody noticed that, either. What's more, Molly leans against the back of the seat, promptly attaching herself to the bus!

I sit there thinking, *Why didn't she feel it or even smell it?* Nobody does. Oh well.

We get to school, and everyone is gathering up their stuff. We all start filing off one by one. And then here comes the screaming!

"Ow! My hair! My neck! Ow! Oh my god! It hurts. No! Don't pull it!"

I am so in trouble, I thought. But this is so worth it.

Well, that is IF they can prove it.

Little known fact, on this particular bus, the cameras don't work. I know that only because I happen to be in the office the day the principal and the bus driver were discussing it. I didn't see any need to share that information with the other kids. I like watching them continue to be on their best behavior like the nerds they are.

The bus driver makes her way to the back of the bus to see what's going on. I get off the bus and walk to the other side, out of sight. I'm kind of under the wheel, but I can still hear pretty good.

The bus driver calls the incident in on her walkie-talkie. Right away, a few teachers and the principal come running. There's lots of murmuring. Then the million-dollar question from Principal Higgins.

"Who did this to you, honey?"

Sob. Sob. "It's. It was Stella. I know she had to do this."

"Stella? Stella Monroe?"

"Yes her! She's evil! She even said she'd wish I die!" Sob. Sob.

I couldn't quite tell who it was, but there were plenty of sighs and "oh my's."

Like to see you pin it on me, though. I smile.

Then I hear the sweetest words, "Call her mom; we're gonna have to cut her hair and clothes. Oh man, look. It's on her skin too. Call an ambulance!"

I heard enough to satisfy me. I casually walk to the cafeteria for breakfast, being sure that I'm not seen.

As I hear the sirens blaring and getting closer to our school, which was quick by the way (they had to have been bored), I find myself actually savoring today's meal. I mean, for some reason, this food just tastes better today. I sit there and out of nowhere, I see staff rushing towards me.

I look up with the look of death, and for the next 15-20 seconds, I nearly feel like I want to throw up! That's when I realized that I left that man in the house to find my goodies.

Jesus! I can't believe I didn't think about that. Awh, man!

As the staff members walk past me, I continue to eat because, well, he's not going to really be looking for anything anyway.

Oh, shoot! Dang it. What about her? HUH!!

I didn't think that part through at all. It was easier when he left her alone for me to do stuff to her.

What if she talks?

She won't. Besides, I keep her so doped up he'd think she was hallucinating being so sick and all.

And just as quickly as the thought came, it leaves. I throw my trash away and head outside until the bell rings.

Outside, I see everybody staring at the bus. Kayla walks up behind me and sucks her teeth.

"Somebody got her good. Word on the street is she said you did it."

"That's called gossip and I don't believe in it."

"Man, you gone get suspended. Might even be expelled."

"How? Where's the proof?"

"You ain't gotta convince me," Kayla said matter-of-factly. "It's the principal and the police you'll have to convince. Look." She points her finger towards the approaching police car.

"That's nothing," I said confidently. "A police officer always responds when an ambulance is called."

Kayla singsongs, "Somebody's getting locked up todaaaayyyyyy."

In the back of my head, I'm like, *I wish they would try it.*

After much screaming and crying, and just as the bell rings, they finally get Molly loose.

My phone vibrates. I walk slowly back into the building giving myself enough time to calm my nerves and answer David. I figured he'd be the only one who would be calling right now.

Oh crap! I was wrong; it's MOM!

"Hi, Mom."

"Hi, Dear. We have to talk. Where are you?"

"I am at school."

"I know *that* but where?"

"I'm just about to walk in the building."

"You need to go to the principal's office. NOW."

"Um. Why?"

"Do not ask questions, young lady! I can't believe what you did."

"What did I do?"

"Your father will be there in a minute."

"Wait. What's going on?"

"You know what's going on. Don't play innocent with me."

"Mom. I swear…"

"Watch your language," Mom says sternly. "You know your father was looking forward to spending time with you. Why did you leave?! If you didn't want to go, you should have said so instead of having me drive all the way across town to watch this Godforsaken woman! What's worse is that you had us worried sick because you didn't answer your phone! What were you thinking?"

Really? Really? Lady, if you knew half the things I did. LOL

"Ok, Mom," I say, relieved. "I'm headed there now."

"Thank you, Stella," Mom says, now in a soothing voice. "You need to have fun. Relax and enjoy this for real alone time with your father. Love you, baby. You know I hate to fuss at you, but when you do something out of the ordinary as this, well..."

"I know," I say again. "I'm sorry. It won't happen again."

"Good."

What a roller coaster!

I slowly walk down the hall wondering what's gonna happen when I get to the principal's office.

I'm guilty of more than just ditching dear old dad. I reach for the office door, and right away I notice all eyes are on me.

Keep cool, I say to myself.

"Hey, dad."

"Why didn't you tell me you were leaving?" David is clearly upset. "And then I get here, and they are telling me you hurt someone?"

There's hurt and anger in his voice, and I couldn't care less. I'm borderline stifling a laugh.

Can he really be that serious? Please.

"But, Dad," I say innocently. "What are you talking about?"

"Principal Higgins said you super-glued someone's neck to the school bus?!"

"What?! What are you talking about?! What makes you think that I did that?"

"You were the only one sitting behind her! You just yelled at her for no reason. And you told her… that… that… you wished she was dead?!"

"Ok, yeah, I did say it. But I was upset."

"Upset over what?"

Now the petty side of me almost goes, *"Because you cheated on my mom. Because you left her for that tramp. Because you ruined our lives. Because you care for that bitch more than your own family."*

But what comes out seems to make me appear more humane than I was aiming for.

"Because, Dad," I say and will tears to come to my eyes. "she makes fun of me, and she knows things that she shouldn't. And she uses it against me when she can. I mean, like some really personal stuff that I never confided to anyone. Molly acts so pristine and perfect in everyone else's eyes."

And right on cue, a teardrop falls.

"Now, she does something to herself," I continue. "And blames it on me! It was the perfect setup because, well, honestly, people would believe her before me, and my attitude hasn't been the greatest lately. But nobody's taking MY feelings into consideration."

Just like that, all of the scathing and scolding looks vanish. I can see hearts melting. All the women in the office cover their mouths. I slump down on the bench and see the frail man once again.

I swear, I need an Oscar or an Emmy or something. I have my acceptance speech together. LOL Never underestimate my powers. If I was old enough, I could sell ice to an Eskimo.

Principal Higgins intervenes. "Clearly this is a case of 'he said, she said,' and unfortunately, transportation is saying that none of the cameras are working today. So, we will just have to accept it for what it is. I spoke to other children around, and none of the stories are consistent."

GOD, could this get ANY better?!!

"So, therefore, to keep down confusion, avoid lawsuits, suspension, possibly expulsion, and any further injuries to anyone else," he says diplomatically. "I think it's best that we put the girls on separate buses and in separate classes. Truly, as smart as Stella is, now would be a good time to consider moving her up a grade."

Dad turns to face me, and I stifle my smirk. It's his fault, no it's that bitch's fault that I didn't move up in the first place. (Another personal thing that Molly knew and teased me about. Secretly, she's jealous.)

It was Karen who said, "Well, honey, I don't think she should move up because she is still young and needs to mature with her classmates." (How, when you are the same age as them? Secretly, I think she's jealous too.)

David fell for it hook, line, and sinker.

Of course, this was AFTER my mom brags to her job about how great I am. I know he and Karen did it to spite my mom. And Karen thought it was the "proper" thing to do.

Jealous bitch.

"Well. Is that okay?" Principal Higgins asked.

Fuck yeah!

"Sure," I say happily. "Dad. I think this is for the best. I know I can do the work and I already have friends in the upper classes."

Principal Higgins smiles and says, "Then it's done. She will get credit for time missed, and I know she can catch up with the rest of the class."

"Great. Let me know if the other child's parents say anything. Since we really can't get to the bottom of it, I'd be more than happy to meet them halfway. Let's go, Stella."

"Will do." Principal Higgins looks at me, and for the life of me, I think he really knows I did it. But with no proof, well what are you gonna do?

Not a got damn thing!

So, now I get to leave school, move up a grade, and not have to look at Molly's perfect little face anymore.

But, the best part is that I get to milk this for all it's worth.

I get in the car, and that sad, sorry man sighs heavily, and it's truly blowing my high right now.

Chapter Eight

Don't You Worry About a Thing

 "Stella, listen," David says. "I know we've gone through a lot and even more so lately. So, I am officially hiring a nursing staff to look after Karen so that you can be a child and do childlike things."

Aw, dang it! Seriously?!

This means no more of the house to myself. AND I gotta hurry and get my house of horrors in order!

Ok. Ok. This isn't bad. Let's let her get better, and I can start all over again — no problem. The agony and torture are fine for me, anyway.

"You should be a happy 13-year-old doing 13-year-old things," David says. "Like having friends. I also think we should go to family therapy. I know the divorce wasn't easy for anyone, including you. Stella? Are you listening?"

"Huh? Yeah. I am."

"I can't tell. You were getting that blank stare again."

"Oh. I was thinking."

"About what?"

"Nothing."

"You sure?"

"Yeah. I am. Too much goin' on, ya know?"

"Yeah. I do."

David grabs my hand and holds it. It's all cold and clammy. It felt really pedophilic, like some creepy old guy who wants you to sit on his lap.

Gross.

I stomach it long enough and am excited when he uses both hands to turn the steering wheel. We drive in silence the rest of the way. We stop at *Momma's House* (not my mom's home, but a local restaurant).

Momma's House is located deep in the hood, and I am quite frankly surprised that he remembers this place.

Oh, he doesn't.

Mom's already here. I'm sure it was her idea to meet us here.

I can't get out of the car fast enough. "Mom!" I jump in her arms. It felt like forever since I had seen her.

"Hey, Pumpkinhead!" She kisses me on the forehead.

I whisper, "I thought you were watching *her.*"

"I was, but then your father asked John to check in on her."

"Oh."

"Yeah. I didn't think it'd be too much, considering she's practically sedated. Your father thought it would be a good idea if we all spent some time together."

David walks up to my mom. He leans in to hug and kiss her on the cheek. I step in and push Mom away.

"Let's go inside," I say quickly. "I'm really hungry."

No, sir. I KNOW what your lips have been on and more than just your "wife."

Mom chuckles. She grabs my hand and snuggles her face in my hair.

"Thank you, Pumpkinhead." She kisses me, and the world feels fine.

I chuckle. David just looks on lost and dumbfounded.

We walk into the restaurant, and immediately all kinds of emotions overtake me. Mostly happiness because my favorite people are there. Tasha, the manager, leaves a table immediately to greet us.

"Hey, Stella! It's been a while since I've seen you, Child! Where you been?" She hugs me.

Tasha reaches out to my mom and gives her the warmest and sweetest smile ever. You can tell Mom appreciates it. Then (the best part), she looks David up and down and says, "Hey."

Boy! I KNOW she just killed him or something in her head.

I like to think she just went *there* with him, including the neck roll. You can definitely tell she wanted to say something. But before he could respond, Tasha says, "Come on. I'll seat you."

"Ms. Tasha?"

"Yeah, baby?"

"Weren't you just serving that table?"

"Girl, that's family." She chuckles. "They'll be alright."

Then that's when I feel it. David is staring at Ms. Tasha's ASS. Like, for *real*! And I know I shouldn't have looked, but I had to know, and of course, he was.

Jesus, dude! What's WRONG with you? Remember when you were a happily married man? Karen changed you!

We get to our table, and David pulls out my mom's chair. Secretly, I think she likes it. It's been a while since he's been nice. Something's up.

I sit next to Mom, and she pats my thigh.

"So," Tasha says. "I know what they want. What can I get you?"

David smirks, and you can tell my mom doesn't like it.

But Tasha gives him that "Boy, don't you even try it" look.

*You know **that** look.*

"Um. I'll have whatever they are having with a beer."

She raises an eyebrow. "Ok."

She walks away, and David is still staring.

I get it. Tasha is beautiful. Long, flowing, natural hair. Nice body. She works out a lot. Light makeup. And smart to boot. Attitude for days! Yeah. I can see why he likes her. But I swear, I want to gouge his eyes out!

Ok, think happy thoughts. I am here with both parents. Let's be civil. The food is ALWAYS good here.

Our plates come and I am trying to figure out how in the world I am going to finish all of it since I ate at school. Tasha must've gotten the vibe David was throwing because Tisha (her twin sister) brings us our food.

They are literally night and day except for their attitudes. But Tisha is way fiercer. When she speaks, you better listen. No one tries her.

I'm thinking that Tasha wants to respect my mom's feelings, but Tisha? Not so much. Once I heard her tell a customer, "Fuck yo' feelings." He was a cop, of all people. Yeesh. She isn't afraid of anyone.

This one-time, Tisha let this guy have it in front of his girlfriend. He must've done or said something awful because before I know it, the words were flying and his girlfriend high-fives Tisha. Then, the best part, the girlfriend dumps everything on him and walks out. Of course, Tisha made sure he paid for all of it. Including a "generous tip."

David notices the switch and says nothing.

Dang. I really wanted to see a show.

Mom and I bless our food and David just dives right in. Being with her has really changed him.

So, no, I don't have any remorse for whatever happens. More of that to come later.

This plate looks so good that I don't want to eat it. Instead, I snap a few pics and put them on Snapchat. Then, the idea hits me. NOT that I want my family back together, but a picture is needed for prosperity.

"Hey, Mom? Dad? Can we get a pic of us all together, like old times? You know, like how when we used to hang out?"

vomit

"Why, sure, Baby Cakes!" Mom perks up quite a bit and I don't like it.

"Totally. I'm okay with that," David says, with a mouth full of food. He's barely audible. I let him swallow first because I need this pic to be perfect.

"Okay! Selfie time! Everybody squeeze in!" I snap about five pics and scroll through them. If you didn't know us, you would think that we are an actual happy family!

I post the pics on Facebook because I know Karen will eventually see them. For good measure, I add the caption, "There is nothing like being with your family."

That oughta boil her blood.

The rest of the time we are there, it's light chatter. Then this.

David clears his throat and addresses Mom.

"I think this is the perfect time to tell her."

"Are you sure? I thought we were going to wait?"

"Why not? Karen. We have to tell her sooner or later. And I'd rather sooner than later."

"So, this is how you break into it?"

I shift at her question. I turn my head to focus solely on his eyes.

"What are you talking about?" I ask.

"Well, honey. With all that is going on, like I said earlier, I have a full-time nurse for Karen. And to make it easy on everyone, we have decided I will have full custody of you so that you can truly focus on school."

There's something in his voice that tells me his mind is made up. This has been brewing for a while now.

There is no way out of this, I think. *And causing a scene will only validate how he feels.*

I turn my head to face Mom. I don't know whether to be angry or feel pity for her. I choose the latter.

As best I can, I keep my cool and return my focus to David.

What was I thinking? There was no need to worry. He would soon regret this. Well, maybe not as soon as I'd hoped, but soon enough!

"You already have full custody. I barely see Mom as is. Are you saying the weekends too, now?"

"Yes. I just think it's best for a while as we go through family therapy for me, you, and Karen. Then as we heal, your mom can be added too. She will also be seeking counseling and parenting classes."

I steady my words.

"Ok. That's it? That's the big deal? Wow," I say, as calmly as I can. "Here I am thinking that you all were getting back together or something."

I grab a piece of bread and start chewing. I have to be as nonchalant as possible. Out of my peripheral, I see that Mom is near tears. So, I break out in song.

Tisha and Tasha say if they didn't know better, they'd think I was Black.

The first song that comes to my mind is "Don't You Worry About a Thing" from the *Sing* movie soundtrack.

Now that I think about it. That is one of the most childish things I could have done. How embarrassing.

And before I know it, the entire restaurant is either joining in or clapping along.

I'm about to go viral!

In the midst, I stand up and dance with my mom. I intentionally move one way or another to keep David from joining in.

Tisha and Tasha are in the back, and all I hear is, "Gone head, baby! Sang for yo' Momma!"

That only makes me be more into it because I love them. They are always there for support.

I finish out the song and David looks at me.

I take a drink of the Pepsi "BeeBop" brought me.

BeeBop is Tasha's daughter and she kept me from committing suicide on more than one occasion and I love her for that. She's super smart, too. She does things so economically that I want to be like her. She does everything on her own and saves a lot of money.

She is taking her "BS" classes (as she calls them) at the local community college and then in another year or two it's off to Howard University!

She tells me about it all the time. She's working to save up money in case of emergencies.

So, I have to admit that was a bit of a stress reliever. But, now back to the matter at hand. And that's devising a plan to make *her* pay.

PAUSE

We'll just call this a mini-break so that you understand the dynamics here.

My father and I have had a strange relationship for as long as I can remember. None the less we were close. I loved him for who he was. A protector and provider. And this is before I wised up.

My mother and I? Well, that bond was always there from conception in my eyes. She is everything and I would literally kill for her. Hmm. Yeah, that part.

Anyway, what they both had in common was that they never held back from me. Even things I should not know – I learned very quickly. Birth control, sex, money, lies, people – you name it – they told the truth. Family secrets are a whole other book.

So that's it. Wealthy family. Loving and close. It was a world that others could only dream of. We were the *American Dream* and now that dream is a skittish nightmare.

Better? More Understanding? I hope so because you will need it in times to come.

END PAUSE

Back to our regularly scheduled program.

Chapter Nine

Defiance

Once things calm down and we are left alone at the table, I decide to pick up the conversation David started.

"Look. We've all been through something because of all of this. My only concern is when will I be able to see Mom since I'll be living with you full time?"

"Anytime you like. Except for school nights and most holidays."

"So, then what's different from how it is now? How will that work? Because I really like spending Christmas with Mom."

"Like I said, it will be a few months of therapy. And we will go from there. Maybe we can work in something like an every other year kind of thing."

"That's not gonna fly," I say before thinking.

"Excuse me?"

"How is it that you will have me practically 365 days of the year and I can't even get what I want when it comes to seeing my mom? A child needs a mother's love too, and it's not like Mom has issues or anything. Outside of being soft when it comes to you."

Mom gasps. "Stella!"

"What Mom? You know it's true, and that's ok. You have a lot of years together. That's to be expected. What's not expected is that I won't be able to see you as much and I don't think that is fair. Why is it that SHE dictates all the rules?"

David's eyes widen and he says, "SHE doesn't."

"Oh, yes she does. And you know it."

"Stella, I am your father, and you have to respect me."

"You – no problem," I say. "HER – fuck no!"

Simultaneously, I hear my parents yell, "Stella!"

I walk off and get in the car.

David pays and Mom follows.

Ok, I lost it a little bit. Maybe a lot but come on! The one real stable thing I have in my life is being stripped away from me.

It's not like my mother isn't capable of taking care of me. I swear mentally I am much better and more equipped to handle things.

David plops in the car, and the tears are streaming down my face. I hate that he is seeing me cry right now. He knows not to say one single word to me.

I pull out my phone and text my mom:

I'm Sorry

She probably thinks I'm apologizing for my misbehavior and disrespecting her. For me, it is more than that.

I put my headphones on and let my thoughts overwhelm me. I am considering my next set of plans. I think about how everyone will pay and the best way to get back at David.

We pull up to his house and I get out of the car. Not waiting for him to open the door, I head straight up to my room.

Sometime later, there is a knock on the door. It's him.

"Look. I know you don't want to talk to me right now and that's fine. I have thought about what you said, and you are right. Disrespectful. But right. I plan on fixing that. I have to leave for work now, but I don't expect you to check on Karen or anything. I already have and she is resting. I have begun an antibiotic treatment. I don't know *what* I'm treating, as I have to respect most of her wishes."

In my head, I'm thinking, *if he decides to draw blood, I'm screwed.*

"Anyway," David continues. "This should help until she can talk and tell me her symptoms and what she was doing before this. I know she was trying some new things out, so I think I can narrow it down. Anyway, until she makes a full recovery, as stated previously, I am hiring around-the-clock nursing care. That way you can be a child instead of having to look after an adult.

Also, I think it's in your best interest if you saw a psychologist. I have set up your first appointment for Saturday." Sensing my reservations, he adds, "If you don't go, there will be consequences. This is to help you. Do you understand?"

"Yes. Yes, I do."

"Good. I'm working late so I won't be home until probably morning."

"Fine."

So, no. I don't check on her.

Instead, I spend my time removing evidence from the house before the nurses arrive. I do leave the cat, though. I just unhook it from the boards and staple it to the wall.

I bag up everything and walk around the neighborhood disposing of the items here and there.

Most of the stuff I just pour out and throw away the containers. No one even notices what I'm doing.

I know my neighborhood well enough to steer clear of the houses and businesses that have cameras.

So, I keep going until the last of everything is gone.

Chapter Ten

Kelsi is Not the Same

 Since I am out, I decide to visit my friend Kelsi.

Now that I get to be a 'kid,' there is nothing better to do. Besides, I am really feeling her brother, Zack. More than Tara's brother. He's 15, and I'm practically 14, so I think we would be a good fit.

I walk up to the door and he answers. "Hey! I was just about to leave and get food. Since you're here, do you want anything?"

"Where are you going?"

"Chinese?"

Suddenly, something about him activates something in me, and I feel a little tingle. If he asked, I would give him my virginity right here on the spot.

"What are you getting?"

"Just rice and rangoons."

"Then I'll have whatever you are. And maybe even from your lips, too." I lick my lips, and I can see him instantly get hard. My eyes follow but still focus on him.

I have no idea of where the flirting comes from, but it is sexy, and I know he feels it too.

Only, he tries to play it cool.

Oh, yeah. I got this down.

Sadly, before we can see where the conversation would go, Kelsi squeals, "Stella! You're here!"

I turn my head in her direction to acknowledge her and then glance back at Zack. "Bye," I say.

"Um, yeah, be back in a bit."

Kelsi pulls me into the house. We head up to her room for girl talk. I like her. She gets it.

"So, how's the slut?"

"That bitch hasn't dropped dead yet. I think she's doing it on purpose."

She laughs really hard, "How sway?"

"Not that she's purposely making herself sick, but she won't die to spite me."

"Oh. Yeah. Well, hell. You could have given her a mercy killing. You are always talking about how she's suffering. But sometimes I think you secretly enjoy it."

I glance up at her, and we lock eyes.

"It's no sweat off my brow," Kelsi continues. "She deserves whatever happens to her for wrecking your home. It's called karma."

I think to myself, *my name is Stella, not Karma.*

Apparently, I find it too funny in my head because I burst out laughing.

"What's so funny?" Kelsi presses.

"Nothing."

"Oh, it's something, alright."

"No, it isn't really."

"Share!"

"I don't have anything!"

"So, what were you and my brother talking about?"

"He's gonna buy me something to eat too."

"Oh. Do you like him?"

"No," I lie. "He's your brother. I can't cross that line."

"You should totally cross that line. I don't like the skank he's with now."

"The problem is my age."

"Haven't you ever heard that old song "Age Ain't Nothing But A Number"?"

"Wow."

"No seriously. He's not a virgin, of course, but you are. That's your in."

"Can you please tell me why you are concerned with my love life and virginity?" I rub my temples.

"Because. You're in high school now. And most girls have to, you know, give it up to the right guy and build that high school love/sweetheart thing."

"While this may be true, I just started high school."

"Which means you're behind. Duh."

"No. Not really."

"Not in classes, silly. SEX! And lots of it!"

"And… why…?" And then it hits me. "You? To whom?"

"Richard. My brother's best friend."

"WHAT THE F…?!"

She cuts me off. "I know. I know. But we have been liking each other for a long time. One day, my brother left to be with his girl. Richard decided to stay, and we first, were just watching TV. Then I went to finish my homework. He played the game. Mom and Dad were gone to work, and it's not like we hadn't been home alone before."

"Dude," I scream. "You."

Kelsi throws up her hand, "Let me finish. YOU HAVE TO SWEAR you won't tell anyone else though."

"I swear." And I won't. She is a really sweet girl.

"So, afterward, Zack still hadn't come home, and I was in my boy shorts and a tank top. He looked at me, and I just knew that was it. I didn't wear that on purpose; it was just comfortable. So, I walked into the kitchen to get a drink, and he came up behind me. Next thing I know he's kissing and licking on my neck. His hands were on my thighs, and then he started rubbing up against me. AND I *LIKED* IT. Every single ounce of it. So much so that I almost dropped the pitcher and glass."

"Oh my god."

She bit her lip. "There's more. So, he let me gain my composure and drink my water. He then took me to the couch. I sat there, and he locked the deadbolt. It was odd at first, but then I realized why. Zack would have to ring the doorbell. Then something in me just snapped. I stood up and led him to my room. He sat on the bed and took off his shirt. I tell you. Those Lacrosse players. Lord, have mercy!"

I'm staring at her in awe right now. She is my new hero. She felt so comfortable to share this deepest moment with me.

"So, we start kissing again, and he's touching me EV-ER-Y-WHERE! My body was on fire! I want it even more now since I am recanting it with you. Anyway, it's getting hot and heavy and deep. So, he pulls me on the bed and makes me feel how hard he is. He tells me, 'This is for you.' Then I got nervous and he must could tell because he stops. But I'm like, 'No, don't stop.' He turns on the TV, and you know HBO After Dark has all those movies playing. Well, we watched like three of them and did almost everything on them. It was like training!"

We both giggle at that.

I need a drink. And I am not talking about water.

I swallow hard, and as much as I think I don't want to hear it, I am intrigued to know more. "So, then what?"

"Well, he told me about how he had to cum, and I will enjoy it."

"What?"

"Yeah. I was like, Well from this point when you enter me, I am the only one. And he says, You've been the only one."

"He was a virgin too?"

"No. But I knew he had one girlfriend before, and they hadn't been together for a while, and I think it was because of me."

"Oh my god. Then?"

"He entered me, and it was *delicious*!"

"Did it hurt?"

"No. I was more relaxed since we did all that other stuff by that time. I trusted him, and I just knew it was gonna be ok. I'm a cheerleader and I've heard all kinds of stories, and none of that happened to me."

"What about birth control?"

"Been on it since I started high school. My mom heard the group talking, and she went and told all the other mothers about what we were saying after one cheer competition. Sooooo, we've all been on birth control since."

"License to kill?"

"More like a license to fuck. Now, mind you. I'm just starting out, but some of the other girls I expect to see in videos and movies when they get older. That's where I learned it from. I mean, when he had me watching those shows, I was like 'Oh, so that's what she meant.' And it was hard to envision the positions they described. Seriously. Between them and the movies, I know a LOT now."

"What about STDs?"

"I thought about that. But he had his physical and checkup. Yeah, we were good."

"Jesus."

"I was like you, but that quickly changed. I know my brother would go for you. Let it come naturally. We are different than kids before you. The world is. I promise I wouldn't bring all this to you if I didn't think you could handle it. You're the only person that really knows."

"What about your mom?"

"Are you trying to get me killed and sent off to boarding school?"

I chuckle. "No. I'm not. You're about the only friend I have. Though, if you're dead – I don't think you have to worry about boarding school."

"Aww." She reaches over and hugs me. She is still sweet, but definitely not the same girl I knew.

We sit on the floor watching TV. I hear the door open and am excited thinking about not only the food but also tasting it from his lips. This newfound information and food make me very happy. I casually walk downstairs, and Kelsi is in front of me, so that helps me gain confidence. I glance at him and we lock eyes, and I get it.

He sets the bags down, and there's all kinds of junk food. Then, my hopes for anything disappear. His parents walk through the door.

"Good evening, Mr. and Mrs. Johansen."

"Why, hello Stella! It's been a while since we've seen you! I am glad you're here. Kelsi, did you offer her anything?" Mrs. Johansen is so much like my mom. That's why I love her dearly.

"Um. Mom. I bought Stella some Chinese. My treat," Zack says, a little too perky.

I knew then he is interested. Ok, well, that is a little awkward because Mrs. Johansen notices too. She smiles, though, and walks off.

The rest of the night, there is absolutely no chance of getting him alone. Kelsi and I finish girl talk and food in her room. I look at the time and realize that David will be home soon.

"Oh, shoot. I gotta go. He will be home soon."

"Why don't you just stay the night and let him know you're here?"

"Half dead lady at home?"

"Oh shit. You're right. Christ! Why doesn't she just die, already?!"

"Wishful thinking."

"If she does, do you think he will get back with your mom?"

"Over my dead body."

"Well, get Zack to take you home. I know he'll want to, anyway."

"Ok. I'll see you Monday."

"Good night and goodbye." She waves me off as if she's done with me for the night.

"Yeah."

She pulls the covers over her head as I walk out the door. I turn off the light and close it.

Chapter Eleven

Zack

I'm walking down the stairs and the TV light is on.

Good, I thought. *I don't have to disturb anyone.*

But the odd thing is, there is no sound. As I round the corner, I see why. There Zack is, rubbing himself and watching PayPerView. I stand there for about two minutes, and then he finally looks up at me. He's not surprised.

Okaaayyy.

He just changes the channel and tucks it back in. "You headed out?"

"Yeah. Gotta get home before David does."

"I'll drive you. It's too late for you to walk."

"Ok."

He grabs his keys, and we head out. We get to the car, and he opens the door like a true gentleman. Once I'm in, he closes the door and gets in. I'm sitting there wondering what it will feel like, even taste like. I got an eyeful when I was watching him.

"So, you aren't afraid your parents will catch you?" I ask when he gets in.

"Why?" He backs out the driveway and heads down the street.

"Just out in the open like that?"

"They sleep like hibernating bears. So no, I'm not."

"Your sister?"

"She's seen enough dick, so I am not worried about her, either. I know her and Richard are together. Anyway, typically at this hour, once she's in her room, she doesn't come back out."

"So why were you–"

"I need a release."

"Oh."

"You didn't seem surprised."

"I know enough," I say.

"Really?" He seems surprised.

"Yeah."

"That comment you made earlier?"

"I meant it."

"We'll see."

"We will."

"You are being awfully brave."

"You have no idea of who I am."

"I see."

He grabs my thigh, and I immediately push his hand further up to let him know I am ready when he is. He knows his cue because he strokes me all over and I swear I am two seconds from asking him to pull over. Then we reach my house.

His car is home!

Oh shit! Moment over.

"Kill the lights before you pull up or I am in deep shit!"

"Done."

He kills the lights and stops short of the driveway.

"I gotta go."

"Wait. I'll come with you to be sure you get in."

"What?"

"It's obvious you aren't going through the front door." He points to the low light in the living room window.

"Yeah. Right."

We sneak through the back gate; I can see my window is still open from the moonlight. Before I start to climb the lattice, he grabs me and pushes me up against the wall. He wastes no time kissing me.

I nearly lose my mind!

I swear the heat in my body just doubles. I grab him, and I rub it fiercely.

There is a little stool by the lattice, and I lift my leg on it to give him full access to me. His hand quickly goes down my shorts, and I gasp.

Oh, god, I want to just give it up now.

He takes his hand out and pushes himself against me and then backs off. He smiles this devilish smile.

"Not yet."

I gasp for air, "Why not?"

"Not yet." He repeats and walks off.

I am left there puzzled.

I know there is so much more to come.

Literally.

Chapter Twelve

Once a Cheater

 I climb the lattice and try hard not to think about what just happened because every time I do, I lose my grip. I make it to my room and creep to the door. I hear moaning, not from the sickly bitch, but like what I just went through. Although, we didn't moan much out of fear of being caught. But it was definitely moaning, and I know she didn't recover in 24 hours.

I'm like, *Ok, there must be something in the air because sex is all around me.*

I half expected to see *Brazzers* or *PornHub* or something like that as I crept up to the stairs.

Oh noooo. The effing golden ticket!

I run back to my computer to be sure that the teddy bear camera on the shelf is still recording. I placed it there hoping I would catch something juicy. And IT IS! They must not have been there long because they were still pretty clothed, but it is hotter and heavier than anything I had seen or felt tonight.

I run back to my room to get my camera. I need good still shots, also. I get back in time to snap some of the best pictures ever. The redhead takes her shirt off and David's eyes light up like a kid who just opened their Christmas gifts. He takes off his pants, and that's when things get really nasty.

She goes down on him like a raving lunatic. With each bob and eye glance, I'm snapping away. It did come in handy to learn what to do, and I absolutely know I will use this against Zack the next time I see him. No doubt about that.

The *coupe de gra*? She takes off the rest of her clothes, and he returns the favor. This is priceless — totally perfect timing. With every position change, I am able to capture it well. He isn't acting like someone new at this.

Which makes me believe that he was a cheater all along even before this other Karen. I make a mental note to ask Mom about it later. And then, in true porn fashion, he lets go in her face and apparently, she is loving every bit of it. The next thing I know, they're turning to head up the stairs. I have never moved so fast in my life. I get inside and hop on the bed. The camera falls out of my hands.

"Stella?"

I don't respond.

"Stella?"

"Do you think she's awake? Did she see us?"

Yes, tramp, I saw you and all your dirty little deeds.

"No. I don't think so. She is a pretty heavy sleeper."

Oh shit! He's at my door!

He peeps in, and I am so still right now. I slowly breathe in and out to imitate rhythmic sleeping.

"I told you, she's out cold even with all your screaming."

He must've hit her on the ass, because there is a loud smack and she says, "Do it again," and moans. "And your wife?"

"She's so sick she wouldn't even know what day it is right now."

"You're a doctor. Why don't do you do something?"

"As if you care. Secretly, I think you're hoping she dies so that you can take your rightful place."

"Well, it should have been me and not her in the first place. Ten years, Dave and I am still the side chick!"

No need to ask Mom; I got my answer now. New mental note: Find out who this bitch is.

"But you're the best side chick a man can have. Don't I treat you good?" He chuckles and nuzzles his face in her neck.

"That's beside the point. Look. I get it, you love them and all, but I won't be around forever you know."

"Just be patient. You will get everything you deserve in due time."

She sure as fuck will.

They head off into his room, and I hear the shower running. I walk in, and Karen opens her eyes.

I walk over to her and whisper, "Right now, your husband is in the shower fucking another woman, and there is nothing you can do about it. He's been cheating on you, too."

A tear streams down her face and her eyes dart back and forth to the shower. She's trying to speak, and I run out of the room because she must've been loud enough for him to hear. I stand by the door to listen.

"Ah, baby, you're up," David says. "Are you feeling better?"

She tries to speak, but the words won't escape her.

"Honey? Why are you crying? Are you in pain? Let me give you a shot of morphine."

Morphine? My ears perked up like a dog hearing the word bacon.

"Why don't you just give her an extra shot and put her out of her misery?" The redhead is anxious.

"That would be murder."

"Who would know?"

"Everyone."

Damn it! Why don't I have a recorder? Oh, wait! There's the camera in their room too. Second mental note: remove all the cameras immediately tomorrow.

I dash around the corner as the two naked ones head back downstairs. I go back to my room to go back into delicious thoughts. The set-up is real and soon. I make plans to ensure that Zack and I will officially be a couple if I have my way. I will get my life back. Real soon.

David must have also found some renewed sense of life. And judging by this new energy and promises, he plans on moving on real soon.

Chapter Thirteen

Just a Day

 The next day, just like clockwork (like before the fake Karen), he wakes up to go running.

Seriously, newfound energy, eh?

So, he should be gone long enough for me to collect my toys.

I take my time, careful not to wake up the precious Karen because who knows what she'll remember when she wakes up.

If she wakes up.

We pretty much stay out of each other's way the rest of the day. Not even for dinner. I leave and don't ask if I can go. I head over to Kelsi's, praying she isn't home, but Zack is.

I round the corner and don't see any of the cars, so I assume they aren't there.

Darn shame. I was in the mood, too.

Oh well. I need to be sure I'm prepared for what's coming ahead, anyway. I hop on the first bus and just ride around the city. I get off to eat and do a little shopping on my own.

Then I find myself in front of *Momma's House,* and I go in. Tisha and Tasha walk up to me.

"Child where is yo' Momma?" Tisha asks.

"Oh. Um. She's not going to be here. I'm kinda alone today."

Tasha chimes in, "Why?"

"Because my dad," (cringe) "is busy and I really didn't feel like making my own dinner."

"Lord. I knew it! I knew this would happen." Tisha throws up her hands.

Tasha wraps her arms around me and I have never felt so much love. "Come on, baby. I will get you somethin' to eat. On me."

"Thank you."

"No problem, Sugar." They always make me feel better.

The food is absolutely delicious and what makes it even more is the hot guy checking me out. He has to be at least 17 or 18.

Here comes that tingle again.

And as if right on cue, guess who walks through the door? Zack!

Dang.

As much as I want Zack, I now want the new guy, too. I didn't think I would like any other race, but I do like this guy. His nice, chocolate skin, melting smile, and brown eyes make a girl want to do horrible things in a delicious way. But then there's Zack and his friends. He notices me and comes over to the table.

"Hey."

"Hey!" I wonder if he senses I was looking at Mr. Chocolate.

"What are you doing here?"

"Eating?" I point at the half-devoured plate.

"I know that. Alone?"

"Would you believe me if I said no?"

"Yes, because then that would mean that you're here with one of your parents."

"I'm not."

"Not what?"

"With my parents," I smirk, hoping he gets it.

"Then you are alone?"

"I didn't say that, either."

Now he's got it. So, he looks around. "Ha. Ha. You had me for a second, but now I get it."

"So slow."

He cocks his head and raises his eyebrow. "Yeah and you'll like it."

Before I can say anything, his friends walk up. I get up, getting ready to leave.

"Where are you going?"

"Home."

"I'll take you."

"But you're here with your friends."

"These fools? I'm sure they can manage without me for a few minutes."

"Ok." I grab my stuff, and we head out the door.

He turns back, and they are giving him the thumbs up.

"I won't be gone long."

In unison, they all say, "We know." And the laughter erupts throughout the restaurant.

In the car, we don't say a word. He just rubs my thigh inching ever so slightly with each pass towards bliss. I remain calm. He must've sensed something because what happens next infuriates me.

"Not yet." He takes his hand away and smiles. Then he takes my hand and kisses it.

I let out a big sigh. "Fine. But let's go on record and understand that I am not the tease here."

"Duly noted."

"I bet." I let out a sigh.

"What is it?" Zack asks.

"Why not?" I blurt out. I throw up my hands.

"Because there's so much that goes into this. I'd rather wait."

"So, masturbating is good for you when it could be you and me? I mean. You brought me to this point."

"Well, for now, I think I would be doing both. I have realized I have an insatiable appetite."

"Oh." I wasn't ready for that.

"Even if we were able to, it wouldn't be enough for what I need."

"You're only 16. Driving on a permit."

"Actually, I am 17, driving on a license. I'll be 18 very soon."

"Wait. What did I miss?"

"I think you always thought I was younger or wishful thinking on your part. So, that means that there's a few years between us. So. Not yet."

"Oh."

In no time, we are home. He kisses me, only less passionate. I get it now. He's waiting until I turn 14 or 15 so until then, I have to be preoccupied and away from him until February. This is going to be a long, hard three months.

Pun intended.

I walk in to see the redhead at the table eating dinner with David.

This is bold as hell. I have to admit; this man has balls. I actually have to give him some respect. (Not much, but some.)

"Hey."

Cue the deer in headlights.

"Oh, hey Stella, Darling. Your plate is in the warmer. Lila made dinner since she knows what's going on in the family. She's a dear friend of mine."

"Oh? Is that so?" I raise an eyebrow.

She wipes her mouth. "Nice to meet you, Stella."

"Yeah."

I just head to my room. For like one and a half seconds, I actually feel bad for Karen. But, like gas, it passes. I close the door and fall asleep.

Chapter Fourteen

Let's Get Her Better and Confessions

 It's morning, and I must've needed the rest because I don't recall getting back up at all. There's an unfamiliar smell.

Bacon! Pancakes?

Is this man cooking? Then, I get a wave of nerves only to realize I got rid of everything this weekend.

Steady your nerves.

Then there's the sound of a vacuum.

Oh, yeah.

The nursing staff is here. I get dressed and go to meet the strangers in my house.

"Good morning," a petite lady with dark eyes says. "I am Alicia. I will be assisting you and your family in the healing process of Karen. In addition, I will cook occasional meals and do light housekeeping."

"Hi, Alicia. It's very nice to meet you."

"I have made breakfast if you would like to eat before you go to school."

"Thank you so much. Um, have you seen my dad?"

vomit

"Yes. He's upstairs discussing with the doctors what the next best course of action is for your mom."

"Stepmom."

"I'm sorry?"

"Stepmom," I say with irritation. "She's my Stepmom."

"Oh. I'm sorry."

I linger around to see what the plan is. David comes down with two other doctors.

The first doctor I recognize is Doctor Davis.

Good Lord. Here's another chocolate man who is so damn good-looking!

I've never looked at him that way until now. The second one I haven't seen before. They are all kind of talking at once.

"Hey, Dr. Davis."

He frowns up a little. "Why, Stella! It feels likes ages since I've seen you. You are just so beautiful and turning out to be quite the young lady. Come, give me a hug, young lady!"

Gladly.

"It's been such a long time! Will you be here for Christmas?"

"Because you asked, of course."

"Good! I will make my famous cookies."

"The chocolate chip ones?"

"Yes!"

"Then that is something I will definitely look forward to."

David interrupts, "Stella. This is Dr. Conway. He is also a specialist. We'll all be referring to each other on Karen. Hopefully, between the three of us, we'll get her better."

"Oh, good. The house hasn't been the same since."

Not if I have anything to say about that.

David continues, "Well, we think that since she's had so much pain meds and other stuff, we're going to put her on dialysis and then start a new regimen. It would take too much to see what the root cause is and by now, we don't know what damage has been caused. Once she's really well enough, we will transport her to the hospital for further testing."

"I think we should do it now," I interjected, for good measure. "Don't you think we've waited long enough as is?"

That was a little too eager. Let's see if they bought it.

They all look at each other. Their faces turn red. Something's in the midst.

Dr. Davis jumps in, "Well, we're just going to try this first."

Then David says, "Stella, why don't you grab your belongings and I will take you to school?"

Oh, that's strange. Do they know or suspect? Remain calm.

"Ok, Dad."

"Good girl."

I grab my stuff and casually walk to the car. I'm running through my head to be sure any and all evidence was hidden well. We ride in silence, and that makes me a little nervous. Then he clears his throat. I jump.

"I wanted to put you at ease as to why we're not taking her to the hospital."

"What is it?"

"Well. I was trying to diagnose her myself, and I might have gotten it wrong. Dr. Davis and Dr. Conway are here to help me keep my license. I think I might have overmedicated her. I should have drawn blood first, but before she got worse, she wouldn't let me. It's going to take a lot of time and money.

"So, we are going to clean her blood first and then go from there. Hopefully, and this is the goal, by cleaning her blood, it will help in her recovery." I won't remind him to take a blood sample.

I was relieved they weren't on to me. He thinks this is his fault (technically, it is). Oh, this is so delicious!

"So," I ask, genuinely concerned. "How are you going to do all of that?"

"Well. We have portable machines that you see in patient rooms. We are going to bring one of those here and do the same thing."

I get it. Clear her blood – clear the evidence.

"Oh."

"I am really sorry this has been a hard time for all of us."

"Well," I began but quickly decide I need to shut up! This is definitely one of those think before you speak moments.

"I messed up, Kiddo."

"Oh, yeah? How so?" I turn on the recorder on my phone.

"Well, for starters, I should have never cheated on your mother. I feel like this is the consequence from that."

You got that right. And Lila's next if I can get near her.

"I am sorry to dump this on you before school, but I have been hiding too much from you as is."

"It's ok. We should have had this talk a long time ago."

"You're right. We should have."

"And Lila?"

"Lila is a longtime *friend* I have been knowing for some time."

Yeah. I got that.

"Anyway," David continues. "She is also a nurse and will be around to help us out."

Oh, could this get any sweeter?

"So, you work with her?"

"Actually, no. I met her at a conference, and she works for another hospital."

"Oh. No wonder I never met her."

"Yeah. Anyway. We are all going to be tag-teaming to make Karen better, or at least try to."

"So, why did you cheat?"

"Well. I don't know why, but I can tell you how it happened."

"We have a few minutes."

This is the first time I've ever prayed that we get hit with red lights the entire time. We've always been able to tell each other anything. The one time having an open relationship pays off. Our conversations have never been this deep, but I am oh so happy it is.

"Well. Before Karen, there was another woman. She and I had met shortly after your mother and I were married right after you were born. We were pretty hot and heavy, too. Your mom wasn't able to be intimate because she had a C-section and was out of commission for eight weeks."

Totally NOT a reason to cheat, but I let him go on.

"Anyway," David continues. "She came up to me after I had a few drinks."

"So, you were at a bar?"

He scoffs.

Yes. I am smarter than your average child.

"It was happy hour, and I was feeling very *frustrated*."

"Oh, please," I laugh. "Just say you were horny."

"I don't think I'm ready for those words with you. But yes, I was. I tried. I really did. I tried so hard to resist her, but she was so hot."

"And Mom isn't?"

"No. Your mother was–is very beautiful. I just had this urge that I needed satisfaction for."

Note to self: When I get with Zack, be sure to fuck the shit out of him.

"Ok. So, Mom's pretty, but you had urges. I got it."

"So, she and I slept together that night."

"Did she know you were married?"

"Yes. That just made it more exciting for some reason."

"Why didn't you just leave?"

"Urges."

"Got it."

"So, she said she wanted to see me again, and I am not going to lie, she practically begged to see me again. It stroked more than my ego."

"I'm sure."

"God, I can't believe I am opening up to you."

"Better for me to know now than later, though."

"Maybe? So, we were off and on and then Ms. Johnson wanted to retire."

"So, let me guess, here comes Karen number two?"

"Lots and lots of people interviewed for that position."

"Soooo, why Karen?"

"She stroked my ego."

"Your ego or your *ego*?" I have to laugh at that.

"She appealed to my arrogance."

"Ah."

"She spoke of how much of an asset she would be. She said she would lend herself to finding new clients, find ways to expand my practice and make more money. She said all the right things for me, I guess."

"Oh, boy."

Red light.

"So, when she came to the second interview, and we panel interviewed her, it was even better. That's when I noticed the subtleties that I saw in your mother. Only, she was younger."

"Midlife crisis?"

"No. God, no. Arrogance. I will admit."

"Oh."

"So, when she started delivering up on what she said, I couldn't help myself. I never came on to her. In fact, she came on to me. She felt comfortable around me. Skirts and dresses became a little shorter, more cleavage, any man's dream."

"Oh, geez." I roll my eyes.

Another red light.

"Yeah. So, here I am, banging three women at one time. Well, not all together, but someone every day. I felt like Superman."

"Superman was a good guy who saved people."

He looks at me.

"Oh, god. Really?" I laugh hard at this.

"Well, there you go. I admit, it isn't right, but it is what it is."

"Thank you for being honest and trusting me."

We make it to school and I get out of the car. I'm not mad. I'm pissed.

He tries to play a sympathy card and on my intelligence. He needs me on his side if this shit goes south.

I got you.

I walk into the building, and it seems so rare and different each time I'm here. I am now a freshman in high school instead of some little eighth-grade kid in some preppy middle school still being treated like some goddamn baby. I round the corner headed to the first hour, and I stop short in my tracks!

It's Mr. "I'm so goddamn fine" chocolate guy! You know. The one from the restaurant?

Chapter Fifteen

Mr. Chocolate

Holy crap!

 I dash around the corner and into the bathroom to make sure everything looks good. I regain my composure and casually walk to class. I look him up and down as he stares at me. I take it all in. He's popular and a jock, a football player. And being the player that he is, everyone wants to be his friend.

Until (record scratch) I see Kelsi.

Dear, God, please don't let this be Richard, the Lacrosse player. Not Zack's best friend. Why didn't he acknowledge him that night?

I try so hard to replay that memory in my head, but all I get is the moment where I would have done anything to give up my virginity and then receiving a "not yet". Clearly, this guy can multitask because while he has his arm around Kelsi, he manages to keep eye contact with me and talk with everyone around him at the same time.

Why haven't I met him? All the functions I've been to. All the times I hung out there. Why haven't I met him? Or better yet, seen him?

I head into class as the first bell rings. I hear, "Byyyyyeee Rrrriiiiiccchhhaaarrrdd!"

Really? Girls still do that?

I find a seat in the middle. I don't want to be noticed yet, and I don't bother introducing myself to the teacher (who is obviously preoccupied, anyway) or anyone else for that matter. I have so much information to process from this morning. I won't say that I feel bad right now because my current soul mission at the moment is to get Richard between my legs.

I know. I know. I said I care for Kelsi, but I need to see why she feels the way she does about him and why I'm feeling the need to find out. I mean, you do recall how she talked about him, right?

So, I slump down in the seat and begin taking notes. Before I can write his name, I think, *if I lose this notebook, what would the person who sees it do with it? Share it?*

So instead, I just start lots of mental notes. I'm deep in thought and don't notice that Richard AND Zack walk in at the same time. I mean, I do see it, but my mind doesn't process it. I guess I was in a trance-like state. But it doesn't keep me from noticing the aroma of Richard's cologne and the soft but quick touch of Zack's hand. Those two sensations combined make me want to proposition the both of them right here and now.

Maybe one day. I hope so.

I won't bore you with the rest of the day because there really isn't much to it. I'm finally in my element. I don't attempt to make new friends, although a lot of girls flock to me during gym, asking all of these questions. I half expect a *Mean Girls* theme but don't find that, either. Besides, I know I'm the true mean girl, and I hope no one finds out the hard way.

The rest of the week is a blur. School, home, then Kelsi's is the routine. Very seldom do I put myself in a position to be alone with Zack. I find myself more entranced by Richard and getting to know all that I can from Kelsi. She's all too willing to share the gory details.

I feel like I'm setting her up. Maybe I am.

But the part of me that would have cared doesn't. We really do have a great friendship, though. Oh, well. Maybe after Zack, I can see if she'd be willing to share Richard.

Make a note of that, too.

Somehow, I feel like Richard is getting the best of both worlds here. Actually, me too. Ok. Works for me.

The rest of the school year goes by fine. I get caught up and even surpass a lot of the kids who've been there the entire year.

At home, everything has gone haywire since Karen stopped working. Things are so stressful. I play my part as the good girl.

Soon, it will be time for my celebratory fourteenth "I'm about to lose my virginity" birthday. At least then I can get away and destress. I book the entire weekend at a hotel using David's card. I convince a guy to check in for me and sign the forms. *Plus, cash always helps.*

I plan everything, and Zack seems down for it.

I tell David not to worry about a party, and he is free to be with Karen the whole weekend, alone.

Karen is getting better. A WHOLE LOT better. With the dialysis and antibiotics plus the nurses' care, she's been improving quite well. This includes therapy for walking and regaining her strength.

Before you get excited, I am not thrilled.

The sound of her voice has gone back to irking me, and she doesn't seem to recall or want to bring up the fact of the little secret I told her. Truly, she should believe her husband tried to kill her. And, remember that he doped her up?

Priceless.

David and Karen have been rekindling their love, and David seems genuinely happy and in love with her again. I thought.

Until one night, I am in the crawl space, and I hear moaning.

Boy, this man does get around.

So, I snake my way through to get a good view of the events. This time, I recognize the familiar face!

OH MY GOD! MOM! (I should be disgusted.) But, boy! Is she giving it to him! GOOD! (Mom's got skills.)

I should be repulsed that she's fucking him HARD in the garage. *Nobody should ever want to see their parents banging.*

Have a little class here, lady.

However, he seems to be enjoying it, and she is, too. Not that I am excited to see them together at all. Did she convince him, or did he convince her?

Either way, not cool, lady.

BUT the fact that she's totally dominating him makes this great. Especially since it is happening in the same house that he shares with his current wife.

Ha! This is golden.

I want to use this newfound information, but not at the expense of Mom. So, I let it go. For now.

I crawl back to my room. As I leave out the door; I find Karen up and watching TV in her room. I casually walk in and sit at the end of the bed.

"Oh hi, Stella!"

"My," I say, caressing the sheets. "You're looking well."

"Thank you. Each day is getting better. I am able to move a little more, and I'm going to the doctor tomorrow for some scans and tests. I realized that some of the holistic stuff I was doing wasn't working."

"Oh, that's good." I turn with a side-eye. "And how are you and (insert pause) Dad? Any plans this weekend? It is like Valentine's Day for you, you know. Since you weren't able to celebrate the real thing and it's the anniversary of you guys meeting. I'll be out of the house and hanging with my friends for the whole weekend. Because you know, my birthday and all."

"Yeah, I am hoping to do something special. Could you help me?"

"Oh, I wish I could. However, your V-Day is *my* B-Day."

"Oh, that's right! Your dad, is he throwing you a party?"

"Mmm, nope. I opted out of it. Instead, I'm spending the weekend with my bestie."

"Oh, good. Maybe I can think of something intimate here."

Good leeway. Thanks!

"Speaking of intimate. How are you and Dad doing? I mean *really* doing?"

She looks puzzled. Good.

"Well, I think that is an inappropriate question, but since you are a little mature, I guess I can share with you that we haven't yet. He wants me all the way better and diagnosed before we can be intimate again. I love him for that."

"Hmph."

"What does that mean?"

"Oh, nothing. Just wondering."

"Wondering about what?"

"Like tonight and a few nights ago, I heard well… Um. How do I put it? You know. And I thought you guys were… let's say… going at it."

"Clearly, as you can see, we are not."

"Oh, ok. Maybe he was watching a movie or something."

"Maybe. Your father is a good and faithful man."

"*Sure.*"

"He IS."

A little anger, eh? Ha. Ha. Delicious.

"Sure, he is."

I walk out, leaving that last statement to burn and linger. She does exactly what I want her to do, use all her newfound energy to go see where her faithful husband is. I must have let the conversation linger too long because as I get back to the crawl space, the conversation isn't what I want.

"Karen, honey." (Adjusts pants.) "What are you doing out of bed?"

"Nothing. I wanted to move around a little. Do I smell a woman's perfume?"

"Oh no, Sweetie. That's probably you."

"No, David. Someone was here."

"Of course not. Why would you think that?"

"Why are you in the garage?"

"It's where I hang out from time to time. Remember?"

"Someone has been here."

"No, not at all. I promise you. No one is here. Look around. Do you see any remnants of anyone being here?"

I do — the used condom under the tire. I do snap a picture of that.

"David. Are you cheating on me? I was on my death bed for months and now on the road to recovery. You can tell me. I'll understand. We can get past it. I love you."

BARF! *That last sentence makes me wretch for real. I mean, it was sick, sad, depressing, and desperate. It ain't no fun when the rabbit's got the gun, huh?*

"Look, Karen," he grabs her hand lovingly and raises it up to her nose. "Is that the scent you are smelling?"

Insert dumb blonde here. Shit.

"Actually, yeah it is. I guess."

All I can do right now is shake my head. He must have a killer penis because the manipulation is real.

They walk back into the house, and I head back to my room. He goes to shower. He comes back out, and I swear he DOES have a killer penis because they did not close the door and I saw it.

And she wastes no time shoving it down her throat. Immediately, it goes from limp to rock hard.

"Fuck it!"

He picks her up, slams her on the bed and pounds her like there's no tomorrow.

I think the extra screaming was for me, as she has never been that loud.

I gotta give her points for that.

I see your petty, and I raise it. I bet I win.

Chapter Sixteen

Birthday Behavior

 Friday night is here. David knows Zack, and so it's nothing when he picks me up alone without Kelsi.

I'm all too eager to get in the car. "Happy Birthday," Zack says and hands me a small box. I open it, and it's a ring.

I let out a gasp, and he places his hand on my thigh.

"Zack, what does this mean?" I ask as I take it out of the box and really examine it. The jewels are small, but they are all real. No cubic zirconium or gold plated.

And yes, he went to Jared!

Here I am with a diamond and amethyst ring.

"Put it on. It's a promise ring I had specially made for you."

"Awwww." I slide it on, and it's perfect.

"I wanted to give it to you before anything else so that you know that it is real between us. I waited for you and everything."

"Oh, my goodness."

He kisses my hand at the red light. "Hopefully, this is the beginning of a lasting relationship."

"Yes, hopefully."

We get to the hotel. We casually walk in with our bags and key cards in hand. No one even bats an eye. I get to the room and…

"SURPRISE!!"

Everyone is standing around talking and drinking and… is that weed I smell?

Oh, yes. Surprise, indeed.

Everyone is a couple. There's Zack and me. Katie and Ryan. Kelsi and Richard (*mmm, Richard*). Devin and Dana. Tristen and Monica. And no one has issues about

PDA or a little action. My first instinct was this is an orgy. Then I think *no, everyone is just ok with who they are.* Although, if orgy is on the menu, I'm going for Richard FIRST.

But it isn't like that. Although I'm practically the youngest one here, no one can tell. I dive right into getting a drink and hitting as many joints as I can. Apparently, this isn't everyone's first rodeo because when they leave, the room is clean and no longer smells of weed. I am really kind of sad about Richard.

Oh, and before I forget, Zack gave Richard his blessing about his sister months ago. It was a few days after he told me he knew. Of course, I told Kelsi.

She told Richard, and Richard 'fessed up'. Zack practically laughed in his face saying that, as long as he treated her well it was ok with him.

Anyway, after everyone leaves, Zack and I are lying in bed, and I have on this cute little negligee Karen never got to wear.

"You look so hot and older, babe."

"It's my birthday, and I want everything to be perfect and special."

"It is because you are."

"Awww."

I turn off the TV and straddle him, kissing him as much as I can.

Oh, he's into it alright. I can feel it. Oh, yeah. I can really feel it.

We waste no time getting into it, and he is gentle and rough at the same time. When he enters me, it doesn't even hurt. When we're done, I slide away looking for piles of blood.

He takes a breath. "Hey. Are you ok?" He cups my face with his hand and looks deep into my eyes.

"Uh. Yeah." I say, feeling silly. "I heard stories."

"Those are from stupid guys who are looking to get satisfaction for themselves and not thinking about the girl. I love you. I would never hurt you like that."

What did he say that for?

"I love you, too." I delve into giving him oral pleasure like I have seen so many times now. From the way we go at it, you wouldn't think this is my first time.

I'm happy I talked my mom into getting me on the pill to "control my periods" when it was actually in preparation for this night. Zack uses a condom, too.

I'm young, not stupid.

Had we not been drinking and smoking, I would have let him enter me without one.

For the entire weekend, we enjoy the pool, sauna, and spa. Every chance we get we have sex and lots of it. Even if I am tired, I never let him know because I am not going to give him the opportunity to cheat even if I was. (Or at least thinking about it.)

Sunday comes, and it's time to check out. We left a DND sign on the door, so housekeeping never came in. We clean up as much as we can, and I leave them a large tip and the keycard on the table.

We go to breakfast at *Momma's House,* and they have a cake waiting for me! The sweet part is that "Happy Birthday" is written in purple heart confetti. Tisha and Tasha always remember my birthday. I love them so much. After that, Zack takes me to my Mom's and I spend the rest of the day there. We just have a quiet day. She notices the hickey on my neck, and I am not ready for the "talk" with her because I don't want to disappoint her. We have it anyway.

"So, you and Zack, huh?"

"Yeah. Me and him."

"I noticed the ring, and I know your father didn't get it. He barely remembers your birthday. He called me to ask the exact day." She chuckles.

"Or, maybe he was too busy getting his brains screwed out days before to notice."

She flushes, "Oh. Yeah. Oh."

I laugh so hard. "It's ok, Mom. Truly, it is. Kudos on the revenge sex, but next time either ALL the way in the house or a hotel."

She clears her throat. "How did you find out?"

"Never mind the details, lady." I laugh. It's comfortable talking to her.

"I wanted that bitch to know how it felt. Secretly, I was hoping she would come down and catch us."

My mom?! The revenge seeker?! Oh, I have newfound respect for her. This poor, sweet, timid woman now has a mean streak? Holy cow!

"Oh, I tried to make that happen." I laugh. "Apparently, he came too fast."

"Yeah. Plus, I had to be somewhere."

"Are you dating? I'm guessing you needed a fix."

"No. Well, yeah. When he called about your birthday, he heard the buzzing. I was so close, and it was really feeling good, so I may have moaned a little too loudly."

"Hmph."

"Yeah. He asked me what I was doing, and I told him. I'm grown. No need to lie, and he offered to finish it for me. It was how he said it. I couldn't say no."

"I don't think anyone could."

"I get there, and it's crazy."

"Oh. I saw you give it to him." She glances at me. "Crawlspace."

"Oh, god."

"No worries, I didn't stick around long. I went to tell her, and she just took too long to get there. She says, 'He's a good and faithful man.' I go, 'Sure he is.' It didn't take long for her to get up and check the house. But he convinces her that basically, she's crazy, and he never would cheat on her."

"She fell for it?"

"Of course, she did."

"Stupid."

"Yeah."

Mom gets up and gets two pints of ice cream. Butter pecan for her and cookies and cream for me. We sit on the couch and finish girl talk while watching *13 Going On 30.*

"Anyway, he goes upstairs to shower, and when he gets out, she starts sucking him pretty good. Then he's pounding her like some animal. It looked more intimate with you than her."

"Oh. He said he still loved me and that he was sorry."

"You didn't fall for it, did you?"

"Of course not. I treated him like he treated me. It was just sex. He's been calling and texting since. He says he's stressed about the house and bills and blah blah blah."

"Yeah. He's been working hard and extra shifts and stuff."

"I know."

"But things have been getting better."

"I know. He kind of asked me back. That's not gonna happen, though."

"I truly hope not. You know he sleeps around, right?"

"Of course not! Well, not at first. What do you know?"

"Well there was another woman before Karen, and then there's this redhead."

"Lila?"

"Yeah. How do you know about her if you didn't know he was cheating?"

"She's the only redhead he knows. He said they were 'just friends'. He met her at a conference and then again at a bar. She's a nurse at Memorial."

"You knew all this, and you didn't think that he was cheating with her?"

"Wait. No. He has?"

"For years, apparently. And even on Karen, now."

"Really?"

"Oh, yeah. Big time."

"Huh."

"Yeah. He's been getting it in."

"You've watched all this, too?"

"No, not much. Just in passing. But obviously, he's got the magic penis."

"Well yeah, he's working with something." (This new information doesn't go over well. She switches subjects.) "What's going on with you and Zack?"

"He and I just became an official couple. We spent the weekend together. I did lose my virginity."

"I'm sure you did. You're way too relaxed about this conversation."

"Oh. I had a good time. It was truly good and relaxing. I was nervous a little. But he was so sweet and comforting."

"I know you are still taking your birth control properly?"

"Yes. And we used condoms."

"Look at you. So responsible."

"Yeah."

We finish watching the movie and Mom takes me home to get ready for school. I hug her and get out of the car.

Chapter Seventeen

She's Back to Her Old Self

 I walk in the door, and David and Karen are sitting on the couch looking so happy.

"Hey."

"Hiya, babe. How was your weekend?"

"It was fabulous."

"Was that your mom's car that I saw?"

"Yes."

Eager McBeaver.

Karen looks up. "I thought she had specified visitations. Why were you over there? Who took you?"

Yep. She's back. And he says nothing.

"Well. It was my birthday, and I haven't seen her in months, and I caught the bus over there."

"And she thought this was ok? You are not grown. David, did you approve this?"

"Listen, it wasn't that bad."

"David, she's 14. *Not* 18."

"Look, Karen, this is her mother for Christ's sake."

"Yes, but we don't need her negativity coming back while I am recovering. Stella has been stellar since she hasn't been around."

"I don't think that's it. I just think she's maturing."

I'm sitting here looking at them have this conversation as if I am not even here.

"David, all I'm saying is we're in a good spot, and I don't want to ruin it."

"Then shut up." Whoa, David. That was harsh. But way to go. Oh, and I know your secret.

That's my cue to just keep walking. I run upstairs to call Zack.

"Hey there," he says.

"Hey, you."

"I miss you."

"I miss you, too."

"How was time with your mom?"

"It was so great. We had a good time talking and eating ice cream."

"That's good."

"I even told her about us."

"What did she say?"

"Nothing. She's cool with it."

"Good. When are you telling your dad?"

"I am never telling David."

"Ok. That's your call."

"Thank you for understanding. Look. Can you get out right now?"

"Sure. What's up?"

"My hormones."

He chuckles, "Oh, yeah?"

"Yeah."

"I'm on my way."

"Great. Climb up the lattice. The window is open."

"Ok."

I get up and lock the door. I added an extra lock just in case. He wastes no time getting here, and I stuff the door and we are sure to be quiet about it, but it still feels so good. He leaves around three in the morning.

This weekend makes me wonder where our parents think we are or what we are doing. Or basically, they just don't care. Either way, I don't care at the moment. I got everything I wanted. Happier Birthday to me.

Chapter Eighteen

Counting Down for Nothing

I get up and get ready for school. I'm a little sore and tired but looking forward to the last few weeks. I'm counting down because I get to spend the summer with Mom. Or, so he says I can. For now.

Zack and I have made all kinds of plans. I will be a sophomore, and he will be a senior this upcoming year. I walk in class and apparently, it must be written all over my face that things have changed because everyone flocks around me.

"Hey, birthday girl."

"How was your weekend?"

"You look different."

"Did you get what you wanted?"

And boy, did I!

Everything has become a whirlwind. Time flies, and just like that, we are in the last couple of days of school. I have been the perfect child. Karen is back to her old self.

Jesus, I hate her, but I love having sex with Zack more. So, I just stay out of their way, lock my door, and have sex. It keeps me from snapping on the both of them. I do my best to keep them from doing anything for me. I even got a part-time job — none of which they know. Zack and I both work at the mall, and I convince my manager to give me the same schedule as him so I can ride with him.

It works, and I haven't had to ask for anything. He also helps with what I need. I wish we could get our own place now. I am so excited about our future, but I haven't forgotten about Richard, either. He and I have become closer due to our connections, and we know so much about each other, including intimacies. We even joke about the two threesomes I thought about.

Me, him, and Kelsi. Me, him, and Zack. Only thing is, I don't think either of them would be willing to go for it.

Sigh.

Finally, it's the last day of school! Yes, Lord! I'm clearing out my locker, and there's a note:

Meet me in the theater. 3:00

I look around for Zack, but he's nowhere to be found. It must have come from Richard. I wait around. Zack texts me that he will be home as he's not feeling well but to stop by. By 3:00, it's a ghost town. The only staff around is the custodial staff.

I slide into the theater and look around. There he is in all of his chocolateness.

"Hey," he says.

"Hey. Where's Kelsi?"

"She left with her brother."

"Then why are you here?"

"Because. I wanted to see you."

"Yeah. This is not a good idea."

"Why not?"

"Kelsi is my friend, and I love Zack. This is a bad idea."

"No one has to know."

"Yeah. And nothing's going to happen because this is not a good look."

"All the joking and flirting," Richard says. "I thought you wanted this."

"First of all, I wouldn't sleep with you in a school setting. Second, it was just harmless fun. I gotta go."

Who am I trying to convince? Him or me?

Before I know it and can get to the door, he's on top of me. He spins me around and presses me up against the door and kisses me hard.

Who am I kidding? I WANT this. I really WANT this.

I give in, and it is pure bliss. I can see why Kelsi is so crazy about him. After we're done, I have him take me to my Mom's to get cleaned up; then we ride over to see

Kelsi and Zack. In the car, we vow not to speak of it. EVER. We agree never to be alone together again.

When we walk into the house, Kelsi jumps into his arms and heads upstairs. Zack and I go to the basement. We already know what time it was. Zack has a cold, but you can't tell. He pleases me in ways I will never forget. We all convene to the kitchen, eating everything we can get our hands on. Sex does something to your appetite just like smoking weed.

Zack drops me off at David's so I can finish packing for the summer. I walk in and there she is, Karen, looking more and more like her old self.

"Who is that?"

"My friend from school."

"He looks older than that."

"He's a junior. Well, senior now. David knows him. His sister is my best friend. So."

"So, you are on a first-name basis with your father now? You are way too young to be hanging with boys like that, Stella. You should know better. It's not a good look for a young lady. Also, I was cleaning your room, and I found your birth control.

"I threw it away because number one, it's not good for you and number two, you shouldn't be on it. Are you having sex?"

"God, no!" I scream. "What the hell were you doing in my room?!"

Luckily, I know she didn't find anything else; otherwise, this would be even crazier than it already is.

"You watch your mouth talking to me like that!"

"Let's get this loud and clear for THE. FINAL. TIME! YOU. ARE. NOT. MY. FUCKING. MOTHER! BITCH! In fact, just stop trying. I let you have David all to yourself so back the FUCK OFF!"

And of course, guess who walks through the door.

"STELLA!"

Aw, fuck!

"Dad! It wasn't me! It was her! Obviously, she's back to her old self now."

"David, I told you her behavior was worse and would regress when it was time for her to be with that woman. She has brainwashed her! Look!" (She throws the pill case at him.) "She's been on birth control and riding with older boys!"

He turns to me, beet red. I go to speak, and he throws up his hands.

"Is this true?"

"It's not like that."

"I bet she's not even a virgin anymore!"

"Stella?"

"Oh my god! Are you *really* doing this right now?" The tears of anger start flowing. (She smirks, but he doesn't see it.) I realize if I want to spend any time with my Mom, I have to keep calm. Then, I think, if I do leave - she will keep snooping until she finds all of my evidence. Can't let that happen just yet.

"And by the way, Stella. I know you had something to do with my cat disappearing."

"Prove it!"

"Did you?" David asks, turning an accusatory eye at me.

"Dad?! Seriously?" My voice is a little high-pitched.

Shit, I forgot about the cat, anyways.

Karen breaks down. *#fake*

Oh, for the love of Christ!

"Honey, what's wrong?"

"My mother gave me that cat before she died."

SWEET!

"Did you not check the pound?" Karen asks him.

"I'm sorry, honey. I didn't even think to."

She's bawling her eyes out. She's got him. Hook. Line. And sinker.

"Look, it's so obvious that we are all emotional. If it helps, I'll stay. I don't really have to see Mom. It's causing so much trouble. I'd hate to come between you two. You won't know that I'm here."

You really won't.

"Fine. Just go to your room. We'll talk later." He continues to console that bitch.

It is now my mission to end this and get out of this place.

In hindsight, I could have just run away. If you haven't picked up on it now – can you see why I hate her now, right? No? Let me show you from another perspective.

Although he poured out his soul to me, what I saw was totally different. She saw David as this up-and-coming and thriving doctor. Meal ticket. Like he said, the skirts got shorter and the flirting heavier. I once saw her rub his junk and he didn't flinch. Another time, her breasts were so far in his face that he turned to lick them. Another time, she was in the perfect position for his hand to go up her skirt. I used to hang with him a lot, so yes, I saw all of this. The ultimate betrayal was when she was down on her knees and his pants were around his ankles. As you can see, there is mutual hatred for both of them.

Since they didn't know I was working (in Illinois you can start work at 12), I had lots of money saved up. Zack and I were already talking about getting our own place. I so hope he was serious.

Because I can't access her health anymore, I decide to start fucking with her mind. Name dropping Lila to start.

I still go to work when home. I just keep myself locked up in my room. They never really bother me, and I move all my stuff to storage.

There is no way she's getting her hands on my shit, including my money. I will cash my check and deposit 75% in the bank and then take the other 25% for food and needs. She goes back to work, and that helps a lot. I start planting numbers. Creating fake emails and emailing him. I know he can't resist, so I get pics from random porn sites to send him. It's creepy, but I have to. I then log into his computer email and leave it open.

Of course, she looks. When she asks about it, he says, "I must've been hacked."

He then fucks her until she forgets.

Then one day, I notice dear old dad has been gone for a while. I stroll down the steps into the kitchen, and I greet them. Things get a little quiet, so I know it has to be something.

"Hey, Dad," I say as I grab an ice cream bar and soda from the fridge that I paid for. I wish she would touch it. "How's Lila? I haven't seen her around in a while."

BOOM

"She's…" He hesitates. "Good."

"Lila? Who the hell is, Lila?"

"A coworker. Nothing big or personal. She helped you get better."

"And she's pretty hot to boot. I like her. She should come around more often." I smile too wide.

Through clenched teeth, "Stella!" (Oh. You didn't confess that to your wife, huh?)

"Oh! Sorry."

I walk away. More like saunter. *Let's get ready to rummmbbbbbllllleeee!!*

In no time, there's screaming and then SMACK!! Rumble, rumble, clatter, tumble, boom, boom, boom. Jesus! HE smacked the CRAP out of her! (There will be a LOT of those who won't get that. LOL But hey, I've been around.)

Ha!

She runs past me crying, and he storms out the door and speeds off in the car. I HOPE he's going to Lila's.

Time to rub it in. I have to admit that she got up the stairs awfully fast!

"Damn," I say while precariously eating my ice cream bar. "What did you do?! Does it hurt?" I reach out to touch her face.

"Shut up, bitch!" She covers her face and slams the door.

"Yeah, well at least I know I am. Plus, I'm not the one who just got the taste slapped out of my mouth. Just admit to yourself that your time is up. Like seriously, he tried to love you, but he just can't. He's a whore. And he loves to fuck. In fact, that night in the garage, he fucked my mom hard and has been begging to get her back since. Check his phone."

She growls, and I go to my room. I need something to take the edge off, and I know it's against the rules, but I call Richard. He's all too eager to oblige. I make sure she knows what I am doing, too. She hates it, every moan and groan and shout of "harder"!

I don't even think that she can be recording it. I can deny it. Say it was a joke. We continue, and she's banging. No, she is kicking at the door!

"What the fuck are you doing? Have you lost your goddamn mind? You will NOT be fucking in MY house! Open this fucking door, or I swear, I will call the police and kick in this door."

We finish, and he disappears as if he was never there. I unlock the door fully naked, and there she is. Standing there. I look at her like, "*What do you want?*

I am still breathing heavy, and it's exhilarating to catch this moment on her face.

"Let's be clear. This is NOT your house," I say slowly. "David has NOT changed the deed. It was my mother's home before your trampy ass ever showed up. I will fuck whomever I want, whenever I want, and if you don't want the rest of your life to be a living hell while you're here, I suggest two things. You either leave or kill yourself. And according to your diary, suicide is an option."

I turn my back and then turn around to face her square in the eye. "Oh! And I did kill your cat." I close the door and don't even bother to lock it. What I do hear is lots and lots of sobbing.

You should have NEVER crossed that line with me.

All summer long I dropped hints of doubt. I tried to get as much as I could about Lila too. She has to be the root of this thing. Skank #1 is what I call her now.

With Zack around, I try so hard to be good; the problem is this family won't let me.

He tells me whatever I'm going through doesn't define who I am or what I can be. Truth is, I'm only with him *because* of this situation.

Chapter Nineteen

Reflecting

School is starting soon, and my plans are slowed a bit. Like, who assigns homework over the summer? I am still working at the mall and my classes are a bit tougher, so that's her saving grace. I wake up to the smell of food, and I hear a faint meow.

Is she tempting or testing me? Didn't she learn from the last time? Ok. Let's play.

I walk downstairs as I know Zack will be pulling up any minute. They learned quickly that the more they try to keep us apart, the more I fight. So, they let me be. More so, SHE lets me be.

I think about this upcoming school year a lot. This is Zack and Richard's last year, and I will be left alone. I am looking for other avenues and trying to be a good friend to Kelsi because she didn't deserve what we did to her.

It's just that I am a product of my situation. I mean, look at me. I had it good even when we didn't know that David was a lying scumbag. He's my father and was a good husband to my mom. How I wish things were different. I really do, but now it's too late. All the skanks that this man has been with has really messed my family up. I sit here and wonder about a lot of this all the time.

Yeah, counseling is helping some, but they can't repair something that has been damaged so drastically and has been going on for so long.

I still hate them. I will ALWAYS hate them.

Oh, and don't worry, dear old dad has his coming, too.

I wish I could be that blissfully dumb and unaware. But you have seen what I've been through so far and I haven't really gone into that much detail. I'll admit it. I am a lost soul. I even went to different churches and stuff.

I'm trying to find my own understanding of God and Karen put a quick stop to that. Which is crazy stupid because she has these holistic approaches and she prayed A LOT when she was sick, sooooo who the hell was she praying to? It's like she wants me to fail and because I don't, this is the result.

As I said earlier, when all of this started, she wasn't that keen on making this family work. Appearances were everything. She would say things like, "I am NOT your stepmother. I am the mother that stepped in."

Really?? Oh really??

For instance, when my mom had a clue, I heard her and my mother arguing over David. I remember it, too vividly. Truly, my mom was waaaaaayyyyyy too nice for my liking back then.

"Hey, um, Karen? Can I talk to you for a moment?" Mom asked.

"Yes," Karen sounded irritated, like she was wondering why my mom was even talking to her.

Yes, she had a key and flaunted around like this was her house. She wasn't a nanny soooo… "Can I help you?"

"I wanted to ensure that everything was okay. I noticed your demeanor has changed, and so has your dress," my mother continued. "As a woman, you have the right to wear what you like. But, as a professional and being around my husband, I would appreciate it if you dressed more on the business side."

"Look. David has not said anything to me about how I dress. If it was an issue here or in the office, I am sure he would bring it up. And, being that it is not you who is signing my check, I'd appreciate it if you address this with *your husband* and not me."

"Well you are in *MY* home, and I am addressing you because I have an impressionable child and I want her to understand value, and you should not feel as if you can come and go and do whatever you like."

"Again, address this with *your husband*. I can't help the fact that you feel insecure about yourself and you are teaching those same insecurities to your daughter."

"Listen. I am by no means insecure."

She stopped her short, "Hmph. Well, maybe you should be. It sounds to me like your husband has wandering eyes. Maybe he is looking for fresher, better meat - so to speak. Maybe your time has run out."

My mom left the office David had set up and what I was proud of is that she left with some dignity. She did not let Karen see her cry. But, when she left, David was still working at the hospital, and that was the first time I saw my mom drown herself in a bottle of wine and cry so hard that she cried herself to sleep. I checked on her often. The last time I checked on Mom before I went to bed, I heard the phone buzz. It was a text from David:

"WHT DID U DO"

So, naturally, I was curious. I looked through her phone. There were all these text messages asking David what was going on and if he was sleeping with Karen. He never responded.

Guilt? Maybe. Possibly the ER was busy that day. I don't know. But I played along and got more than what I bargained for.

WHAT DO YOU MEAN? I texted.

KAREN HAS THREATENED TO QUIT.

WHY? I pushed.

BECAUSE OF UR STUPID ALLEGATIONS.

IF SHE IS REFERRING TO ME ASKING HER TO DRESS MORE APPROPRIATELY IN MY HOUSE WHAT IS WRONG WITH THAT?

SHE SD U SD MORE THN THT.

LIKE WHAT?

U CLLD HER NAMES.

Now, considering this was a grown-ass man who is a DOCTOR, the longer he texted, the more it looked like I was talking to a high schooler.

I CERTAINLY DID NOT.

He then sent a screenshot of where my mom supposedly sent Karen all of these messages:

U FKG SLUT.

LEAVE MY MAN THE FK ALONE.

Karen - MRS. MONROE. I ASSURE YOU I AM NOT DOING NETHNG W/ UR HUSBAND. IS SUMTHG WRG?

YEAH. I KNO U R SLPG W/ HIM IRL. I'M NOT FKG STUPID.

Do you see the pattern here?

First of all, my mother GRIPES ALL THE TIME about this type of texting. She talks bad about HER friends who are on social media and type this way. She enunciates and pronounces every single letter and syllable in every word. And he thinks she has done THIS? A prominent teacher? Seriously? He is totally 31 flavors of dumb.

Turned out, while Mom was upstairs, that bitch must have grabbed her phone and sent herself these messages.

I will spare you the rest of the back and forth screenshots that he sent of the "argument."

DAVID. REALLY? COME ON? I WOULD NEVER DO THAT. CHECK THE SPELLING. I AM A TEACHER, FOR CHRIST SAKES.

THT IS BESIDE THE POINT. SHE IS NOW SYG SHE IS GOING 2 QUIT. I DNT HV TM 2 FND ANUTHA PERSON. R U GNG TO HANDLE THT?

I DON'T BELIEVE THIS.

He sent another screenshot — this time of the messages from her to him. What he didn't crop or leave out was:

"MYB I SHLD QT, SO THR WNT BE NO GLT."

Also, on the screenshot was half a picture of her in what I assumed to be lingerie.

I responded back in what I think could be the best Mom impression.

BABE. I JUST MISS YOU. MAYBE I DID GET CARRIED AWAY. IT WAS A BIT OF A STRESSFUL DAY, AND I

HAD A FEW GLASSES OF WINE. I MISS YOU Ok? I REALLY MISS YOU.

His response:

WHTEVR TTYL

And that, ladies and gentlemen, was the day he ceased being my father and I knew she would pay.

I started to delete the messages. Then I realized that it would be great for her to see. She could finally see him for what he was, a man-whore. I sat the phone down next to her, hoping she would wake up before he got home. It didn't happen.

IN FACT, there was Skank #1 with him. Like, seriously? I didn't understand at the time, but I left it alone. I didn't know. I only recall now because I'm telling you. How could I have suppressed that?

They are sitting on the couch like nothing is wrong.

I say ok. (And give it no other thought.) I go back to my room.

A little while later, I heard him coming up the stairs. I peeped out my door, and I saw that his pants were unbuttoned, and his shirt was off. There were even scratches on his back.

I thought, *Mom? Or her?*

He walked over to the bed and goes, "Shit." He is looking at her phone.

Yeah.

He picked up Mom's phone and opened it up. At first, I didn't know what to think. Then it hit me. He was deleting the text messages!

I was pissed.

I heard the shower running, and I dashed in there and grabbed his phone. I forwarded all the messages between him and Karen to me. In the end, I guess I wanted to spare my Mom. I really wanted to send them to her, though.

Luckily for me, I have fast fingers, so I was able to forward everything he had before he got out of the shower. I sat the phone back like it was and the water shut off.

I made a mad dash back to my room. I laid in bed trying to steady my breathing. He came in to check on me and kissed me on the forehead. I wanted to strangle him right then and there.

I knew whatever was going on, I was going to sabotage it.

Chapter Twenty

School and the Holidays

School starts without a hitch. I lay low, devising a new plan. I'm the good little girl — the overachiever, in fact. I make it a point to avoid Richard at all costs. Of course, I do see him every now and then because, well, we're at the house together. I make sure to stick by Zack. Kelsi never leaves us alone. Sometimes, I wonder if she knows or has a feeling. If she does, she never lets on. I join a few activities to keep me busy when I can't be with Zack. Richard tries several times to get us alone, even at school, and for those times I have enough excuses to last me decades.

I swear, time is flying. The holiday season is among us. First, there's Halloween. I buy candy and pass it out. I don't bother to decorate or dress up.

I'm not in the mood to be at stupid high school parties or walking around, begging for candy. It's a nice, unusually warm night out, and I decide to sit on the porch for hours, flipping between social media and Netflix and responding to "Why aren't you here?" texts.

I look up in the sky, and the sun is just about to set. The red, orange, yellow, and purple hues are magnificent. Off to the left, on the horizon, I can see the moon rising as well. I snap a few pics and enjoy the view.

Neither one of the "adults" bother me, and for this brief moment, I'm peaceful. Children in the most adorable and elaborate costumes come out from all over the neighborhood. Sometimes I hide behind the bush and jump out, or I sit on the steps or on the swing on the porch.

God, please keep those children from going through what I went through. Don't let them lose their innocence like me.

I even pray for me. To deliver me from this.

Candy gone. Going to bed.

Then there's Thanksgiving. They make BIG plans, and none of them include what I want at all. But ALL of her family is here.

"Where's Mom?" I ask David.

"Stella, come on now. You know better than this." He seems moody.

"Well. What do you mean? Isn't she family? From what I understand..."

He throws up his hand. What? You don't want me to tell your secret? *Again?*

"Again, don't you think that this would be awkward and hard on Karen? She's just recovered."

"Like literally all of *HER* family is here and just a few of yours. And I have not really been around any of these people."

He lets out this deliberate breath. "Fine. Why don't you go to your room, then?"

That's your answer? Go to my room? What am I, nine? You're right. I will go to my room.

And out the window, I go. I head over to Kelsi's, and she opens the door, excited to see me.

"Stella! OMG! I was just about to call you to tell you Zack was on his way to come get you!"

"Well, I guess I beat you to it."

"Yes. You did!"

"You look so pretty."

"Thank you. You do, too! I wish you wore makeup more often. Zack likes it that you don't. But I think it makes you look absolutely gorgeous. Come on in. There are lots of people you know here. And we have a surprise for you!"

Oh, god. A surprise? She knows better than this, but as I round the corner, I realize it's the greatest surprise a girl could ever want!

"MOM!" I rush to her, and she grabs me up as if I'm nine and hugs me so tight. I am thinking of how embarrassing this is, being fourteen, but I honestly don't care.

"My god. You are aging. I feel like you are growing up and I am missing all of it." Tears start to form in her eyes.

"Oh, come on Mom. It's ok. Really it is."

She wipes the tears, and the smells that hit me are ones that I would recognize ANYWHERE. As I look up, there is EVERYONE that I love and that loves me.

Zack is there, of course (he has red roses in his hands), Tisha and Tasha, my mom's friends and coworkers, and Richard! It's such a wonderful moment, and they are all here for me. The only one missing is Judith, but I understand it's all because of her religion and know she loves me, also.

Kelsi walks up behind me and wraps her arm around my shoulders. "I am so happy you were able to ditch. I had been planning this for months, and I just didn't know how to get you over here to celebrate with us."

"You could have just asked."

"True, but you know we talked about *that* party and how you had to be there. You know? For show?"

"Yeah true. But that didn't last long."

"I see that!" She squeals and up walks Zack.

"Hey, babe."

"Hi."

"These are for you."

"Thank you."

"You look so beautiful. I am glad you are my girl."

"Thank you. Me too."

"I hope you are hungry. We have lots to eat."

"Actually, I am. I'm starving. I haven't eaten all day."

At this point, you should know that I'm trying to change but, well... I'm just not there yet. And I poisoned and drugged everything I could. Every chance I got. Yeah. All my old tricks. Except for the cat. Not yet, anyway. Let them eat, drink, and be merry. Assholes.

We stand around the table and bless the food. Richard secures his spot on my left and Zack is on my right. Mom is next to Zack.

I like this. I like the fact that Mom is okay with him and me. Kelsi is to Richard's left. It's great — especially when Richard ever so slyly rubs my thigh, back, and butt before grabbing my hand. We both play it off so well. That tells me that he's still interested. All while prayers were being said, he keeps squeezing my hand. I make a mental note.

All the men step aside to let the ladies fix their food first. Then we sit at the beautifully decorated tables. This night cannot be more magical. We sit, eat, and drink.

Yes, even the teens have moderate glasses of wine. After that, the men go to watch TV, and the ladies are cleaning and making to-go plates. I step into the backyard and walk out of sight behind a tree to reel it all in.

Okay. I cry — a LOT.

The tears flow so hard and fast. I miss this world — this life. It's a much easier life. I don't want this night to end. I just want to go home with my mom. I need her.

I guess I must've been crying really hard because I don't hear Richard until he touches my hand.

"Hey. Are you okay?" Barely audible from the pie in his face.

Just like a dude. He has a slice of what looks like Tasha's famous peach cobbler and a napkin balled up in his hand. He swallows and licks his lips and even in all of that, I see remnants of pie on his lips that I want so bad.

"Yeah. No." I let out an exasperated sigh to steady my breathing.

"I get it. It's overwhelming? Everyone here for you. I don't know everything, but I can sense the other home life isn't that great. Well, considering that night."

"Yeah."

"So why doesn't your mom fight for custody?"

"She did and lost. It cost her a lot of money. Although she is well off, this custody battle thing nearly drained all she had. Plus, that man has great people in his pocket."

"Aw, shit."

"Yeah."

"I really am sorry."

Are you? Because you haven't put that pie down yet. In fact, you're inhaling it. But hey, it is good pie if Tasha made it.

He finishes the pie. Before he can wipe his face, I grab him by the neck and kiss him hard. I taste all the butter, sugar, cinnamon, and pie crust. He drops the plate and pulls me in close. We finish just in time. He picks up the plate, and since there is no need to wipe his mouth, he hands me the napkin to wipe my face.

Up walks Kelsi.

"Hey, you two! My two favorite people." She stops short, and my heart stops.

"Why is she crying? What did you do to her? What did you say to her? Are you being a jerk to her?" She is pounding Richard hard in the chest.

I'm like, *shit, ok she didn't see us kiss.*

Richard doesn't know whether to run or let her continue to pound him. Guilt, I guess. His little brain hasn't caught up to the fact that she doesn't know.

"This is supposed to be her day! How could you ruin it, you jerk?!"

He's still speechless.

I find my voice. "Kelsi! Kelsi!"

I grab her arm before she delivers another blow. "He didn't! In fact, he made it better. I was crying before he got out here. He was talking to me and gave me the napkin to clean my face! Calm down!"

She turns beet red from embarrassment.

"OMG! Babe. I am so sorry! I just thought. I don't know. I'm sorry."

He now gets it and barrels over laughing. "It's okay. I now know not to piss you off."

"Hey, can you run up to my room and get my make-up kit? She can't go back in looking like this."

Like a good boyfriend, he leaves. Now, the ruckus stirs Zack, who walks past Richard with a glaring eye. Richard averts his attention and continues to Kelsi's room. Zack then locks his eyes on me. Did he see us?

"Hey."

"Hey."

"What are you doing out here alone?" His tone is so low that it was scary.

"I needed. I needed a breath of fresh air."

"And Dick?" I think it's a deliberate play on words.

"I was crying, and he was comforting me."

"Really?"

"Yeah."

He turns to Kelsi for confirmation.

"Yeah. I thought he was the reason she was crying. Turns out she just misses her old life before. You know."

His demeanor changes.

sigh of relief

"Come here." He hugs me so tight. All I can do is cry even more. They love me. They get it. And here I am with Richard, doing this to them. I make a resolve for sure this time to NOT let Richard near me or touch me again.

Richard comes back with the make-up, and we all sit around in the moonlight while Kelsi fixes my face and gives my eyes time to clear up. The eye drops help. She wants to be a stylist and designer, so I also let her change my hair. I look so pretty when she's done. There are two braids that swoop up into a bun.

We walk back into the house, and all is right with my world.

"There's my girl!" Tasha grabs me for instant selfies. "Do it for the Gram, girl!"

All of a sudden, there's lots of SnapChats, Twitters, and IGs. I'm in heaven. I never pick up my phone once.

The night ends. I hug everyone. Each hug feels tighter and tighter like they will never see me again. Mom agrees that she will get me later to see Judith. I thank the Johansens for hosting such a lovely evening. Zack gives me one of his jackets, and we head home. I finally decide to look at my phone. There are a lot of text messages from *them*.

We sit in the car, silent at first, and then he speaks.

"Hey, listen. Is everything okay between us?" Whatever this is, he's hesitant.

"Yeah. Why wouldn't it be?"

"I feel like I rushed you into things."

"You didn't. I wanted to."

"Well, you know. I'm 18 now."

"And shortly, I will be 15."

"I know. Now that I think about it. It feels odd."

"Odd how?"

"Just odd. Like I took your last bit of innocence odd."

"Well," I chuckle. "You kind of did."

He grimaces. "I know. I always wanted to be with you. But I really wanted to wait longer."

"Yeah, well. That didn't happen. Besides, I planned a lot of it, anyway."

"I know. It just feels strange now."

"Please don't ruin this. Where are you coming from?"

"Well, I noticed that more guys are in your face."

"It's ok. Really, it is. And you mean Richard?"

He pauses. "Mainly."

"He's your best friend. Do you think he would intentionally hurt you or Kelsi? Do you think *I* would?"

GOD! I really am my father's child.

"Well. It's just tonight. I saw you."

My words have to be slow. "You saw what?"

"I saw you go behind the tree. Then moments later, he came out. He stood there eating his pie. Then he disappeared behind the tree with you. I was frozen. I didn't know what to think."

"Well. Don't think," I say and grab his hand. "Richard was just being a good friend and a listening ear. He gave me a hug. That's all."

"Yeah?"

"Yeah."

He lets out a sigh of relief, and we pull up in the driveway.

Chapter Twenty-One

Spill the Tea

It feels odd. Most of the lights are on, and there are faint lights trailing off. I still never look at the text messages. I walk up to the door and wave Zack off. David answers and he looks shook.

"Yo. Dude. You scared me," I say.

"Where the hell have you been?"

"With Zack," I say and point back to Zack who is pulling off. "They asked me to come over for dinner when they found out I was sent to my room."

"Did you do this?" He is shook. Never mind the fact I snuck out the house.

As I walk closer into the room, there is a pungent stench of vomit and feces.

Yes. Yes, I did do this.

I look shocked enough. "How can I do something I wasn't here for? I've been gone all night!"

"Stella, nearly half the guests got sick. Two had a severe peanut allergen, I can't even recall the other two allergens, half of them started vomiting and shitting EVERYWHERE, and Karen has had some sort of relapse!"

Oh. My. God! Things worked out better than I planned. They won't be back for a LONG TIME.

"Not at all! That's crazy! I wasn't here."

"Well, it's so convenient that you 'weren't here,'" he mocks. *(Was there a need for air quotes?)* "So, all of these people just got sick, huh?" (Oooohhhh, his voice is gruffy – scary – NOT.)

"I don't know what to tell you, but I am not the bad guy here."

"I swear. I feel like you are out to get me!"

Ding, ding, ding, ding, ding, ding! Tell him what he's won, Johnny! But then again, with all the shouting, the neighbors are looking. This could go any kind of way.

"No. I swear to you. I…"

"Just go to your room and STAY there this time."

I take the cobbler that Tasha made with me. No way is anyone touching it. In fact, I take all the food with me, including the plates made for him.

About an hour or so passes, and I hear cleaning. I creep to the steps to see a cleaning service scrubbing the house from top to bottom. I must've fallen asleep. I go back to my room. Odd thing, David isn't around. Then I remember he must be at the hospital. I sit on the bed and turn on the TV. There's a knock on my door. The cutest Spanish voice bellows through.

"Miss. Would you like your room cleaned? Miss?"

"One second." I get off the bed and unlock the door. "How did you know I was here?"

(For those who don't speak Spanish, or for those for whom it's been a while since your Senior year in high school, I'll translate for you.)

"Su Padre, Señorita."

(Your father, Miss.)

"Que dijo él?" She seems shocked that I speak so well. But I can tell she appreciates it.

(What did he say?)

"Que estabas aquí y no te molestaría. Y no limpies tu habitación."

(That you were here and not to bother you. And don't clean your room.)

"Estaba durmiendo, y no tienes que hacerlo si no quieres."

(I was sleeping, and you don't have to if you don't want to.)

"No es molesto. Parecía un poco idiota cuando hablaba de ti. No me gustó. Nadie debería decir malas cosas sobre su hijo."

(It's no bother. He seemed a bit of jerk when he talked about you. I didn't like it. No one should say bad things about their child.

"Que dijo él?"

(What did he say?)

"Que eras un niña malo. Hiciste enfermar a todos los huéspedes al envenenar sus alimentos. Él simplemente no puede probarlo. Haces cosas malas."

(That you were a horrible child. You made all the guests sick by poisoning their food. He just can't prove it. You do bad things.)

"Muchas gracias, pero no necesito los servicios. Pero definitivamente debes cobrarle más y gracias por decírmelo."

(Thank you very much, but I do not need the services. But you should definitely charge more and thank you for telling me.)

"Lo entiendo y no hay problema."

(I understand and no problem.)

Ok, the gloves are off.

Chapter Twenty-Two

The Last Holiday Together

 Christmas comes, and I tell David that there is no need to decorate or buy gifts. I'm over it. The tension is so thick you can cut it with a knife. I promise you this, I want to ruin it for them now, but in due time. In due time. I'm building my evidence, and David can't let go of his ways. Every time I get my hands on his phone, I find a new woman in his messages. I send everything either to my email or phone.

Karen takes it upon herself to spend lots of money on Christmas. The house is decorated beautifully. This time, they're watching me like a hawk. They stick close together while preparing the food.

Everyone recovered, and she has to practically beg them to come back for Christmas. So much so that she and David spend tens of thousands of dollars, like withdrawing 401K and going into my trust fund dollars, to make this happen. They NEVER leave the kitchen once preparation starts. They sleep downstairs as if I would be *that* petty to ruin gifts and decorations.

LMAO okay, actually, I would be. So, take that smirk off your face.

I pack my bag and head over to Mom's. I figure they won't miss me. And they don't. I spend the entire winter break there, and there isn't one text or call. Mom says that David called once to see if I was there. He never tells Karen. But that isn't the whole conversation either. It seems that dear old David wants a Christmas gift from Mom. She says unless he's paying for the Hilton or higher, not a chance in hell. He hangs up. I imagine he contacts another one of his skanks.

Good for you, Mom.

Christmas morning, Mom and I wake up to cook a small dinner for Kelsi and Zack. We laugh and drink. By the time they get here, we're a little tipsy. They can tell. But we have a good time, anyway. Zack and I go for a walk around the neighborhood. By the time we get back, it's time for them to go. It's such a good night. The next few days, I just lounge around my mom's place while she is at work.

It's New Year's Eve, and I am so excited. Mom lets me spend the night at Kelsi's. We bring in the New Year drinking and popping fireworks. It turns out Mom has a little secret of her own.

She has a man and his name is Jonathon!

And from what I hear, he's really good to her. I mean, *really* good to hear! I can't be happier. It is great. I want her to bring in the New Year with him. I think she's not ready to let me know yet. That's okay. She should be happy. Zack and I stay in his room, though this time, nothing happens. We just enjoy bringing in the New Year together.

The next day, I go back to David's, and they are getting ready for work as I walk through the door.

"I swear the little whore acts like she owns the place, comes and goes as she pleases. Having sex. And he says nothing. I only manipulated him into getting custody so that it looks good for both of us; plus, I got tired of the back and forth pick-ups. I am so glad I have two years left of this little bitch, and then I get to kick her out. I hate her!" As she turns around, she gasps and drops the pot of coffee and her cell. Her mouth is open wide.

"It's ok," I say coolly. "The feeling is mutual, but you could have really just left me with my Mom. It really would have been better for you."

I say it so calmly that it scares me. I walk off as David comes barreling down the steps.

"Stella! What did you do?!"

"I startled her. But not on purpose this time."

I glance back to see that she was still in shock and actually bleeding and blistering.

David calls back. "Hey, get my medical bag."

"Nope." I go upstairs and shower and get dressed. Zack is waiting.

By the time I'm dressed and ready to go, she's all bandaged and still quiet.

Oh, god, you should see the fear in her eyes right now.

I walk off without a word. I get in the car and close the door.

"Are you good?"

"Yeah. I am."

"Anything happen?"

"Yeah. It did."

"Well, what happened?"

"She confirmed everything I felt."

"Okay, you are being too calm and cryptic. Even for you."

I repeat Karen's rant verbatim.

"Oh, shit," he says when I finish.

"Yeah. Oh, shit." I smile, and he says nothing the rest of the way.

Secretly, I think he's afraid of me, also.

Chapter Twenty-Three

Familiar Faces

 So, we have this freshman mentoring program and guess who is nominated as a member?

It's hardly ever that they recruit sophomores. It is usually reserved for seniors to serve as liaisons and mentors. The program is ever-evolving and now it has become a *thing.* They think it's best that we recruit those who have walked in freshman shoes recently. I played the model student a bit too well. So, now it's time for me to be a mentor. And guess who I get to mentor? MOLLY! I have to teach her how to counsel and groom her freshman mentee.

Did you forget about her?

The little skank thinks she is a mean girl and all. She comes in like she is already running things. Then, when she walks in and sees me, she goes pale white.

I never miss an opportunity to rub it in.

I can't believe all this time we haven't seen each other. Mainly because we ran in different circles, I assume.

"Welcome, freshman! I know you have been in school for some time and it's actually almost over, but we are recruiting new members and want to show you some ins and outs of what we do and have been doing for our school community! I am excited, and you should be also. I'm Stella, and I am one of your coaches so that you, in turn, can coach others. Please. Have a seat, and we will begin shortly. Be excited! You get to skip class all day and eat like the Gods!" I say.

I show them the display of food and her gaze drops. She doesn't know how to take me.

That's a good thing, but I decide not to mess with her. I need a good positive record for what's about to happen next.

The day goes without a hitch. Molly finally warms up to me. This time, she knows better. She knows just what I am capable of, even though she still can't prove it. (I can faintly see the scars on her neck.) I really think she thinks it's all behind us. And it is… for now.

School day is over, and I am exhausted mentally and physically.

I head to David's house. The idea of Karen being there infuriates me. I can't wait to graduate or end this – whichever comes first.

Two more years, right? Wrong. Wrong. Wrong. Wrong. You, Lovely Karen, have until the summer, or else.

I won't do anything until after my birthday. I want so bad to end this so quickly. All she had to do was leave my mom and me alone. But, no! She just HAD to be vindictive and mess with my family. She had to mess with *me.* I did nothing to her. She did it to my family. She started this. Why would she do this? If it were not for her, I would be closer in grades to Zack. In fact, we would be graduating together, as I would have skipped two grades. How often does someone get that opportunity? She started it. And I'm going to be the one to end it. #EmotionalWhirlwindedThoughts

It's April! It's my birthday!

And it's ruined before it starts.

Number one, once a month, it sucks being a girl. And this is the start of it.

Two, for the past few weeks, Karen has been steering clear of me, but her words are still everywhere. I saw it in text messages and emails to friends and David. Posts on Facebook about how miserable I am making her. "Just venting," she says. Everyone is taking her side. *Man* is she covering her ass.

All of them saying how she knows I made her sick and killed her cat. David is loving and caring but should be doing something to me. Counseling is not working. Blah. Blah. Blah.

It's laughable because I truly have been quite the opposite. All I do is go to work and school. I am number three in the school ranking. I am a mentor. No discipline issues at home or at school. I haven't even griped about seeing my Mom.

I walk down to grab something to eat and drink from the cabinet before Zack comes over. I'm preoccupied with my thoughts. I go to reach for a cup, and instead of it just jumping and leaving, it attacks me. (I did not notice it sitting on the counter. I didn't even do anything.) I mean *seriously*? I almost feel like she trained these cats to hate me.

I swear I have steered clear of it and it of me. I mean, there is no reason for this cat to be spooked. I wasn't even that close to it.

Why was it even on the counter, anyway? Disgusting little beast.

So, now I kill my perfect attendance because I'm not going to school looking like this on my birthday. That's bullshit. I call Zack to let him know.

"Hey."

"Hey."

"How close are you?"

"I just left the house."

"Okay, go straight to school. I'm not coming. The cat scratched my face, and it is bruising pretty bad. Plus, it's bleeding. I might need stitches."

"Oh, no. Are you okay? Do you need me to take you?"

"No, I'll be fine."

"Okay. Text me later. Love you."

"Okay. Love you, too."

"Bye."

I grab a few napkins and head upstairs. Guess who sashays down the stairs at the same time? And she has the nerve to chuckle.

Was it a nervous chuckle? Is she happy I'm injured? I'm thinking to myself.

I honestly can't tell. But she chuckles nonetheless and says nothing else. So, that tells me that she wants what's coming. I go to the bathroom to assess the damage. It's bad. Really bad. To the urgent care, I go. I grab my bag and insurance card. I grab a towel to hold up to my eye. No way in hell am I letting David touch me.

David comes out of the room as I head down the steps.

"Stella. Are you okay?"

"Yes. Actually, I am." I'm trying to get out of here.

"What's wrong with you?"

"Nothing!" Instinctively, I turn around.

"What the hell is wrong with your eye?"

"The cat attacked me! I was reaching for a cup and didn't see it on the sink."

Cue coffee cup falling and gasping.

Karen begins calling Beauty the cat and grabs the crate. I promise if I wasn't bleeding and in pain, this would be funny.

"I'm okay. Really."

"Where are you heading? You can't go anywhere like that."

"I know. I am okay. Really, I am."

"Are you sure? I just need to grab an ice pack and my bag." He reaches out to me.

"NO! Don't touch me!"

I run out the door and make a mad dash around the corner. This thing of David being a concerned father doesn't work for me. Luckily, Urgent Care is around the corner. I sign in and wait for my name to be called. I tell them I'm pregnant hoping this will have me seen without a parent or guardian present. So far it works. If I had gone to the hospital, they would have called him for sure.

"Stella? Stella Monroe?" The nice but portly nurse smiles as she sees me walking up. "What did you do to your eye, honey?" She cups my face in her hand. She looks so concerned. So loving.

"Not me. My stepmother."

I may or may not have left off "cat" accidentally on purpose.

"What? What did your father say?"

"Nothing of concern."

"Oh, my. Do you feel safe at home?"

"Define safe." I air quote with one hand. I grimace as she takes the towel further away.

"Maybe we should get the authorities involved."

"No. No. It was our first altercation. And I'm sure it will be our last. Things were just out of hand."

"Sweetie, I've been in the business for years. This is how it starts. She will continue to hit you if you let her."

"I promise you. It was just this time. Please don't say anything. My dad is pretty well known. I don't want to get him in trouble."

(Insert puppy eyes. Hook. Line and sinker. Can't have her messing up my plans. Even if it is for good intentions. She just may be a material witness for later.)

"Well, alright. I will let you go this time, but if I see you again, I am going to have to report it. And trust me, I'm single, my kids are grown, and I work all over the city. I'm sure I will see you if you decide to go somewhere else. Believe me." She completes taking my vitals. "Ok now, let's take a look at your eye. Ouch. That's bad. Maybe we should get the authorities involved."

"No. Please don't. It would be bad for everyone. Especially my dad. Besides, everyone would think I had it coming, especially with all the things she's been saying on social media about me."

"That's the thing darling. This is how it all starts."

(Shit. I'm losing her. Think! Got it. Start crying.)

"Alright, honey. In the end, it's the doctor's call, but I warn you. Let me see or hear of it again, and I am reporting it myself."

"Yes, ma'am."

The doctor comes in. "How are we… Ouch. What happened?" He grabs my face, and his hands are so soft. Not to mention, he is so good-looking. He's definitely

Asian. I can tell that from his accent. And his accent…
#Sexy. His smile melts my heart. His eyes invite you to
do whatever he asks. His dark, short-cut hair is
absolutely dreamy.

"My, my."

"Her stepmother's cat scratched her."

WTF is the lady psychic? Nice guess.

"Yeah."

He's turning my face left and right. "Hmm, yes. You will
need stitches. Nurse Becky. Please start prepping her.
Where are your parents?"

"At work."

"So, you are here alone?"

"Yeah."

"Why didn't they come with you?"

*Because you probably know David and there's no chance
in hell I'm letting him near me.*

"So, who signed your medical treatment forms?"

"I did."

"How old are you?" He picks up the chart to examine. "Oh, you just turned 15. Ok. What a bum of a birthday, huh?"

"Yeah."

"I am going to treat you, but I will have to get your dad on the phone."

I'm in pain and looking up didn't help. As if on cue, I get a text from Zack:

I didn't go to school. Call me when you're done. I'll come get you.

I text back:

PLAY ALONG DR STUFF

"I can call my dad," I say and call Zack instead.

"Hello?" (Where did that bass come from?) We'll talk about that later.

"Hi, Dad? Yeah, at the urgent care. They need to speak with you."

Cue the registrar on time to complete the final steps of registration. I grab my ID and insurance card out of my pocket to hand to her.

"Sure, honey. Do I need to come down?"

"Um, I don't know. You are on speaker."

Dr. Handsome clears his throat. "Hello, Mr. Monroe. This is Dr. Pak. I am here with Stella, and she is going to need stitches. We need your consent to treat."

"Of course. Of course. Do I need to come down?"

The registrar chimes in. "Typically, we would say yes, but if you can't get here, can I fax it to you?"

Dr. Pak chimes in, "I am in agreement this time. However, this cannot happen again."

"Sure. Sure. Here is my fax number. 217-555-7673."

"Thank you. We can fax it. Just please send it back as soon as possible."

"Sure. Will do."

The registrar takes my information and leaves the room.

"Alright. That will work. Thank you, Mr. Monroe. Ok, Stella. We'll get started. You will need someone to drive you home." (Why can't Dr. Pak just take me home?)

"That's ok. I can walk. I literally live around the corner."

"No. I don't feel comfortable with that, either."

"Okay. My cousin can come get me. He's 18 and my dad will vouch for him."

"Okay. Before we get started, I need to be sure they will be here."

"They will be."

I text Zack again:

COME GET ME UR MY CUZN WHEN YOU GET ME

He texts me back:

K

"Ok done, Dr. Pak. He's on his way."

"Good."

Nurse Becky comes back with a small pill. "Here, honey, this is a painkiller. Then, we will basically deaden under your eye. And then you will get your stitches. By then, you should only feel a little pressure. Also, you will be a little loopy."

"Ok." I pop the pill like I've been doing it all my life. Ten minutes later…

Woah. I wasn't ready for it. I don't need anything else. I'm nearly gone. I remember lying on my back and then seeing string or thread and Dr. Pak talking away.

I'm out of it. Obviously, he isn't talking to me. Then, another person comes in and says, "Her ride is here."

Dr. Pak looks up for a second. "Good because she is really loopy." He looks down at me and winks his eye. "All done, Stella. But we are going to let you lie down for a while. Do you need anything?"

"No, Sir."

Nurse Becky rubs my arm. "Alright, honey, you did very well. We're going to let your cousin come and sit with you. Here's a blanket. You may get a little cold."

"Thanks."

She walks out. A few minutes later, here comes my knight in shining armor. He looks so worried, but he has a little bag in his hand. He waits until we were clear before he speaks.

"Hey. You alright?"

"Yeah. I'm a little out of it. But yeah. Thanks for being here."

"As if I wouldn't be?" He bends down and kisses my forehead. I fall asleep.

I wake back up, and he's playing some game on his phone.

"Hey."

"Hey there, Sleeping Beauty. How do you feel?"

"Much better."

"Good. Let me get the nurse."

Before he can stand up, Nurse Becky walks in. "Jesus, girl. I gave you half a pill."

"That was half a pill? Don't do drugs, kids." I said with the drunkest chuckle.

"That's right." She pats my shoulder. "I placed an ice pack on your eye while you were sleeping. It looks good, considering."

"Awesome." I touch below my eye.

She hands me a card. "Here's my personal number. Call me if you need anything."

"Thank you." I slide her number in my pocket and walk out with her. She hands me some chips and a bottle of water from the counter. "Eat this. It will help you feel better."

Zack walks up with a wheelchair. This attention is crazy. He wheels me to the car. I get in and wave back at Nurse Becky.

Chapter Twenty-Four

Bye, Bye Beauty

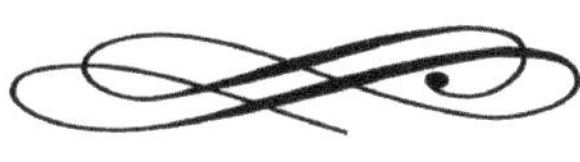 We make it home after a quick drive around, and I am wide awake. I am looking for the cat and I am furious. Zack has to go back and get Kelsi and go to practice. No one is home, so this is going to be quick. The cat is lying on the couch.

As swift as I can, I took the hammer off the mantel and hit it in the head.

Checkmate, bitch.

I take it down to where Queen Sheba is. There is blood dripping as we go. Karen will be home first. But I look at the clock, and there are about three hours before she does.

The trail is deliberate. But not the final resting place for this one. I just want Karen to follow the trail to see Queen Sheba. Then come out to look for Beauty.

I go back and grab a bag to throw Beauty in. Then, I stuff her in my backpack and leave with a hammer and a few nails. I walk down a few streets. As usual, avoiding being seen. I find the perfect spot to dispose of Beauty. Beauty has suffocated now, and I nail her to the pole. Then, I dump the bag, hammer, and nails in the dumpster of the local store next door. I walk away before being seen. I go to the school to hang out. I text Zack to let him know that I'm there.

He meets me at the parking lot. With the same small, little bag in his hand, he hands it to me and smiles. I open the bag and inside are the most gorgeous pair of Dolce & Gabbana sunglasses.

My God! He really loves me!

"I got these as a part of your birthday gift. I guess they really came in handy now, huh? They'll be good to cover your eye."

"Yeah. I guess so." I throw them on. They match perfectly with the outfit I had changed into. (I threw away the outfit I was wearing, too.)

"Happy birthday, babe. With you looking this hot, I gotta take you to dinner."

"Mmmm, food."

"Yeah. I figure you should be hungry."

"I'm starving."

"I bet."

He goes back to practice, and I head to see how many teachers I can run into to get my homework and assignments I missed. I get so many hugs not only for my birthday but also for my injury. By the time I finish, I get almost all my teachers except for two and those classes don't really matter.

I meet Zack at the field (no one is allowed inside during practice), and he is all sweaty and stinky. It is still fairly cold outside.

I look him up and down. "Let's get to the car before you get sick. You should know better than to linger outside in the cool or cold when your clothes are wet." He tries to hug me. "Eeewww – you stink!"

"So, you won't hug me?" He laughs.

"Ew, NO."

He laughs again, and we head to the car. Kelsi and Richard are leaning against it. They smile and wave. Kelsi runs up to me, and she goes off about the cat.

"Kelsi. Really, it's ok."

"Ugh! If it were me. I swear, I would do everything awful to that cat."

I look at her over the rim of the glasses.

You have no idea, Kelsi. You have no idea.

"No. If I did anything to that cat, I would be in serious trouble."

"Then let us do it!!"

"NO. God, no!"

Zack unlocks the door and opens it for me. Richard does the same for Kelsi. We all pile in, and boy, do these two stink! We get to Zack and Kelsi's. They both shower and change. Richard does, too. I think he purposely walks past me in the towel. I avert my eyes. Kelsi looks in bewilderment.

The boys are complete gentlemen. They take us to Maggianos. The guests and host look at us like they know we are about to start trouble. We order and have such a pleasant time. The food is delicious. The manager compliments us on our manners. This kind of life suits us.

After, we head to the movies and pick a random one to see. It's empty, and each couple chooses a different side. We kiss and cuddle and enjoy the movie.

It seemed like everyone is waiting for us to misbehave that day, but we are the exact opposite. In fact, the manager gives us free tickets to come back because of it. Once she finds out it was my birthday, she gives me another set. I guess because it was a slow day or she was in a generous mood. Either way...

I'll take it.

Whenever I am with them, I never check my phone. Truly, none of us do. I get back in the car. It's 10 PM. I check my phone, and there are 12 missed calls and 13 texts split between David and Karen.

All of which basically ask about the blood trail, Sheba and Beauty, and urging me to come home. NOW. As if I'm taking *that* bait. I tell Zack to swing by the hotel we stayed at. I made friends with one of the girls at the front desk, and she lets me use David's card to check-in and get a room. I tell Zack that I will be waiting if he comes back, but I need to rest. Plus, I don't want to go home yet. I have the whole week there. They all decide to stay the weekend.

I give them the room number and tell them that I am turning off my phone. On David's dime, I enjoy the spa and room service. This is some *Home Alone* shit. I decide to find it on PPV. I sit there and relax. I'm not going back to school until my eye heals, anyway. I also know the police will be waiting for me. The fool never even thinks of checking his credit cards.

I disconnect my phone. I take the battery and SIM card out. Zack calls every few hours until we meet up. I just walk around and no one bats an eye at me the entire time I was there. I eat breakfast. Work out. Sit in the sauna. And then go back to the room.

Finally, the weekend is here and Zack comes up later, and we sit on the bed and just talk. Sex slows down because he feels awful. I tell him not to, but I think it strengthens our relationship. Or, so I think. I know he loves me. But it seems to me he may be concerned with who or how I am.

That weekend, we all stay in the room, eating and drinking. We don't cause trouble and just have pure fun. Mom calls Kelsi to ask if she's seen me. Kelsi tells her that Karen hit me, and boy, did the sparks fly. My mom hasn't cursed in a very long time. Kelsi also tells her that I just want to be left alone for a while. My mom buys it. She asks us to text every once in a while.

Done.

Chapter Twenty-Five

Back to Hell

The weekend ends, and Zack takes us all back home. Zack drops me off first. We pull up to the house, and they're both there. They must have known that the time was coming for me to come back. I walk in the door, and here it goes.

"There she is! Call the fucking police!"

"Karen, calm down."

"She killed both of my babies!"

I stand there looking at her. I don't know what is on my face, but it convinces David that I'm innocent.

"That little bitch has got to go! She is ruining our lives! She made me sick. She killed Sheba. Now, she killed Beauty!"

She charges at me. David jumps up and grabs her.

"Calm the fuck down. She didn't do it."

"Yes, she did! I know she did! She told me!"

She breaks down and starts crying. What follows is a laundry list of all the things she found that I planted. She confesses how she knows he has cheated on her, but it's ok because they can work it out and it's time I get out. Maybe send me to a home or back to my mom. I am "ruining everything".

"She did this!" She stands up and grabs photos off the table and throws them at me. I pick them up and see Sheba practically decayed and falling off the wall. There are flies all around Beauty, and people are taking pictures. Glued to her head is the word BITCH used from newspaper clippings. In the back, I peer and see she had posted flyers!

Priceless. I promise you; I nearly gave myself away from wanting to laugh.

I just open my mouth in shock and then frown.

"That fucking bitch! She ruined us! She ruined you! If it weren't for her, you'd probably still be married! You said it! Multiple times." A vein pops out on the side of her head.

Secretly, I'm hoping she's about to have an aneurysm the way she is panting, screaming, and looking like she is about to pass out.

He grabs her. "But then I would never have met you."

Insert pause and deer caught in headlights.

He must've realized what he said, and he literally drops her and runs to me. The tears roll almost immediately, and I hate myself for letting them see me cry. I expedite my plan. They both will pay. I swear to God with every fiber of my being, they WILL PAY.

I turn to make a hasty exit.

 "Stella! Stella! Wait! I didn't mean that. Stella, honey, wait!"

He's tripping over everything and even up the steps. I'm too quick for him to catch me. I bolt my door and push the dresser in front of it. I don't bother to sneak out. I just sit there crying and crying and crying, oblivious to the fact that Zack crawls in the window.

Apparently, he heard the commotion and came up to see if I was ok. He must've been at the door about to knock or something. Good for him that he didn't use the front door. He never left. In his hand is the bag for my glasses.

He grabs me by the shoulders and shakes me. I don't respond.

"Hey! Stella! Talk to me!"

Barely a whisper. "He thinks everything is my fault."

"Why would you say that?"

"SHE said it. THAT BITCH! She said it and his words to her were 'then I never would have met you.'"

"He what?!" Zack is fuming.

"Don't worry about it. I'm ok. Let me pack some fresh clothes. I will just go stay at my mom's."

"Ok. But this is not over." He flops on the bed looking at me.

"No, it's not. But the fight is not today. She has control over David and he is a sucker for her. I am exhausted with all of the back and forth with her."

I stay at my mom's until things cooled down. I must admit the time with my mom is so rewarding, but I couldn't stop thinking about getting my revenge and getting this whole situation over with permanently.

David calls to ask me to come home so we can talk and work things out. I oblige. I happily oblige.

I think that by going to worship with my mom and her new boyfriend, Jonathan, I'll get better. I don't. I can't. All I can think of was what I would do to these two next. And with David calling me to come home? Made it all the better. I really did want to change. But not yet.

I try. I learn so much. I try. Even Zack, Kelsi, and Richard come with us. We look like the perfect, happy family. But all I can think about was getting back to David and the wicked stepmother.

My mom doesn't like it. She didn't want me to go back to David's House of Horrors. She doesn't want me to come back at all. Especially since he hadn't really been asking about me. Maybe she thought they had some type of trick up their sleeves. I play the role even more.

(You know.) The good girl.

No more sex. The whole nine.

Chapter Twenty-Six

Trying to Change – Old Habits Die Hard

 Jonathan shares a lot of scriptures with me, and it's like having a personal talk with God because everything he says, only one person knows besides me. And that is God himself.

I try. I want to try.

Even Richard and I officially break off our thing. Kelsi admits to turning her life around. We are all doing well in school, at work, and with extra-curricular activities.

I try. I want to be good.

I get to David's, and things change. Quickly I might add. I had only been gone a few weeks. It seems they've been going to counseling and couples' therapy before I got back. Hence the reason they want me back.

I don't bother going through the door. I don't want to see their face or deal with them. I climb through the window. The dresser is still in front of the door.

I move the dresser, unlock the door, and begin to climb back down. It would be really strange for me to just walk down the stairs as if I had been there this whole time.

Then something catches my eye. There are another set of prints on the window. I crawl back in and start looking around. Wouldn't you know it? She has been in my room. My bed has dirt on it. My laptop is ruined. I can see water stains all over it and the screen is busted. There is bleach all over my clothes in my closet. All of my pictures are cut up in the drawer. She had a field day in my room. (I guess I had it coming since I killed both of her cats.) I get to my secret spot. It is untouched.

I climb down, and I am not even mad.

Touché. So, you do have it in you. You wanna play? Let's play.

I use my key to let myself in. They're having dinner.

"Hey."

David perks up. "Hey, Stella. Have dinner with us."

"No, thanks. I ate before I got here."

"Oh. Ok."

"I'm going to head to my room if that's ok?"

"Sure. We can talk later."

I peer at her. The smirk. She thinks she got away with something, but I already know. I just play the part.

I walk up the steps and then to my room. I don't cause trouble. I know I had it coming. I don't even wait. I come back downstairs and start grabbing boxes and trash bags. David looks at me quizzically.

"Stella. Are you moving out?" He laughs jokingly, but it still stings, nonetheless.

"No. It seems all my stuff is damaged, so I have to throw it out. It's ok. Most of it was old, anyway."

"Wait. What do you mean? Your door was locked."

"Yeah, and your dresser was in front of the door." She stops short because well, how would she know? Unless she was in my room.

Oh, really Karen? I look at her. Now the face of fear that I love is back.

David looks at her.

"It's weird. I know. But, like I said, it's ok. I'm in my last two years, so I will be revamping my look, anyways."

"I'm sorry. Let me help you with that."

He calls the cleaning service, and they come out right away. He helps me bag everything and throw it away. She knows better than to protest. A part of me still wants him to beat her like he did the last time. But I will take this, for now. The cleaning crew does a great job. We literally get rid of everything. From that point on, my room is bare. I don't add posters or anything — not even a TV. I just do everything on my phone.

The rest of the school year I'm even more of a model student. I'm the best kid. Even David and I have good moments. Summer comes and I work overtime. I make sure not to be at home as much as I can. She lets her guard down. Apparently, David has even given up his women.

Or, so I thought. I get home early one day. And wouldn't you know …

I know for sure that David should be at work. I know Karen is. But I hear it. All of it. And, sure enough, he's back to his old tricks. Plus, a few new ones, as there is a white powdery substance on the table. Should doctors be doing that? They are so far gone that I get some explicit pictures.

He's still out of it when Karen gets home. I sit on the couch and watch TV. I can tell she's contemplating speaking to me.

"Stella? Where's your father?"

"Downstairs. I think."

"Whose car is that?"

"I dunno. I thought you would. Besides, I am not his babysitter. That's your job." I flip through the channels with arrogance.

"Hmph."

Yeah, hmph.

She heads downstairs. What happens next is so unforgivable. There lies David and Skank number whatever (I lost count at this point) in their birthday suits. And that glorious powdery substance on the table. No need to display them now. Not yet anyway.

"WHAT THE HELL, DAVID! Who THE FUCK is this?!"

I can only imagine that they pop up and now he has no excuse. Nothing. She *had* to know he was going to cheat on her again like he did to my Mom. With her.

The girl rushes past her and runs clean out the door.

She's naked, and her clothes are in a ball — keys in her hand. Chirp. Chirp. I guess she's driving home naked.

LOL.

The next thing I know, there's that rumbling again. They're fighting. She's screaming and cursing, and he's talking about divorce, and he is sick of her. *That* I manage to record. She runs up the stairs, crying, and to their room. Only, she trips over her feet and comes tumbling back down the stairs. (Okay so maybe it wasn't *her* feet, but, well, she did trip. So there's that.)

Holy shit!

He's dressed, and there are scratches all over his face. Dang, somebody's been to self-defense classes. He's wrought with guilt. I just stand there and look. He tells me to call 911. She's unconscious. I casually do so. They get there in no time. Is crime that low? Are they really that bored?

Was today a slow day and they needed action? There are two police cars, a fire truck, and an ambulance. Of course, they ask questions, and it's taking everything in me to not tell everything. I'll wait. He convinces them enough that she fell on her own and off to the hospital we go. Had they went through the house – there would have been big trouble.

I go with him to the hospital. I sit there in the waiting room. He knows most of the staff, and they don't seem shocked, nor do they call the police. Dr. Hamilton walks up and shit hits the fan. David walks solemnly towards him.

"Kyle. How is she?"

"She's stable. What the hell happened?"

"We got into a really bad fight."

Up walks the Original Skank. (You know, Lila the "friend".) She pulls off her surgical mask and gloves that are covered in blood.

"Hey, everyone. Stella. Um, Stella can you please go have a seat over there?" She points to a few seats that she probably thinks are out of earshot. But, wait. Why is she *here?* I thought she was at Memorial? "We couldn't."

Dr. Hamilton turns to face David. "Did you know she was pregnant?"

I stand up like Michael Myers after being shot in the face. This is about to get good.

"Wh– Wh– What? She was pregnant? Wait… *was?*"

This can't get any juicier!

The Skank addresses him by name instead of doctor; there's venom in her words. He did marry Karen instead of her, after all.

"Yeah, David. (Scoff.) It was a boy. He didn't make it. She was far enough along to know the sex, but not far enough along to ensure his survival."

Dr. Hamilton raises an eyebrow. "That goes back to my original question. What the hell happened? You're scratched up. She has a black eye and bruises."

"We got into a fight over my infidelity, and she ran up the stairs and fell."

Ohhh, the smirk on Lila's face. I caught that, Ma'am.

"Did you hit her?"

"Of course not! Those bruises must have happened when she tripped on the steps."

"She *tripped*? And got all those bruises?"

"Yeah. I swear."

LIAR!

"Well, I won't get the police involved, but I can't speak for anyone else on the staff. You know, this doesn't look good."

He walks away.

Lila steps in and barely whispers, "Maybe it's time for a divorce and a new start in a new city. You have a history here. You may want to get a change of scenery."

Good one, Lila. This is your chance now, right? But if he didn't then, he probably won't now.

Chapter Twenty-Seven

Road to Recovery – Part 2

 A few days go by, and she's home. He's so wrought with guilt and afraid she's going to go to the police. She's different. Depression full on. She barely gets out of bed. I go and sit with her, not out of concern but pure enjoyment. Taunting her was the best part. I know she doesn't want me here.

Today is different. Today is the day.

I tell her what Lila said to David. I ask her how she felt about Lila taking care of her. Then, I lay pictures of the other women and their devious acts in front of her. I open her bottle of pills to be sure she has no problem getting to them. She just cries even more. I place a glass of wine laced with Fetinol on her bedside table.

Yes, I still have access.

She takes about five or six or more pills (I know I saw at least that many) and inhales the wine. I wait patiently for her to drift. I wake her up, knowing she's out of it, and tell her she's forgotten to take her medicine, so she takes five more with another glass of wine. This is it.

I'm over it, and I'm going to have a good last two years of high school. I wait. I watch. She's having trouble breathing. In the meantime, I steal her diary. (I had perfected her handwriting months ago.) I write her suicide note, and it sounds just like she wrote it. I wait some more. Like three hours. When I check her, she is cold. Barely breathing and with a low pulse.

Finally, I call Mom.

She sounds happy, and I hear Jonathan in the background.

"Hey, baby! What's going on?"

She's so happy. I hate to do this to her.

Cue hysterics.

"Oh my god! Mom! I think. I think she's dying! What should I do? She's not moving! She's so cold! She's dead! Why does God need another angel in heaven?"

The tears mixed with "God" should secure my spot with Mom.

"Oh, honey. Hush now. It will be alright. Sometimes things happen for a reason."

Yeah, like her screwing up the family.

"I'll be over soon. Bye."

"Bye, Momma."

"Hey, you need to call 911. Now."

"Ok."

Immediately hanging up the phone, I stop crying. Everything is coming together nicely. David will be home soon. Time to end this. I take the syringe and fill it with Dilaudid and Fentinol. There is no regret.

No remorse in my heart.

I move quickly to a sleeping Karen who is having an excruciating time breathing.

Why hasn't she died already? Probably too ornery to die and trying to spite me. This should be the final blow.

I inject the entire content in between her toes with the intent to end her life. As the last of the mix is pushed into Karen's body, she opens her eyes to see the hate, deceit, and betrayal in my eyes. Before Karen closes her eyes for the final time, I smile at her. The same smile I gave when I defeated the cat.

Moments later, once I'm satisfied that Karen is dead, I return all of David's medical equipment, get rid of the gloves and take a shower. Then, it's time for the call.

"911, what's your emergency?"

I begin crying. In between sobs, I speak, "Hi, please help! My stepmom isn't breathing. I don't know what to do! My name is Stella Monroe. I live at 1301 Tower Road."

"Ok, honey. Stay calm. Help is on the way."

"I just checked on her. Her body is so cold."

"How old are you, sweetie?"

"I'm 15."

"You're going to be ok. Are you home alone?"

"Yes. My dad is at work. At the hospital."

"Have you called your dad yet?"

"No. But I have another phone. Can you hold on?"

"Sure." Being sure the operator can hear me; I call David.

"Hello?"

"Oh, Daddy! I need you home now! Mom isn't breathing. I called 911."

His first clue should have been that he knows I really wouldn't call her mom in the first place. But hey, he buys it.

"What happened?"

"I went to check on her, and she wasn't breathing. I gave her CPR, but she didn't respond. I hear the police coming, but you have to come home."

"I'm on my way."

I imagine David frantically packing all his belongings and rushing home. He must be panicking. His heart pounding hard so he can barely think straight. Tears flowing. I know he must regret leaving me home alone with Karen. How can he expect me to bear so much? Or maybe his fear is that I did it.

I return back to the 911 operator, knowing that all is going according to plan.

"Hello?"

"Yes, darling. I'm here. You performed CPR?"

"Yes! But it didn't work. My dad's a doctor, and he teaches me a lot because I want to be a doctor, too."

"Wow. You are such a brave young girl."

"But it didn't work."

"Was she sick?"

"Yes, Ma'am. She was severely ill once. Then she lost her baby and fell into a deep depression."

"The police are there. Can you open the door?"

"Yes, Ma'am."

I hang up and walk slowly to the door. Every second that they don't get to Karen is another second to confirm she's dead. Still crying, I open the door and the female officer takes my hand and moves me to the side. The paramedics on cue (or instinct) go up the stairs. They already know all hope is lost. (Or at least that's what I am hoping. But hey after the dispatcher relays the information that I gave, how could they not?) The paramedics stay up there (just bring the dead lady, please). I assume they are trying to revive her. The female officer sees the paramedics coming. She pulls me in for a close hug to shield my view of Karen's lifeless body. Oh, no. I WANT to see this.

I push myself free from the officer, run over to the gurney, and grab Karen's hand.

"Mom!" (I want to vomit saying that.) "Mom! Mom!" I shake her as if, at some point, there will be a response.

The way I am acting one would think I am sincere. Damn, I should become an actress, instead.

I am so believable that a third paramedic gives me a sedative to calm me down.

Oh, shit. I didn't see that coming.

As they prepare to leave, David pulls up. You can tell he's been crying an awful lot. His eyes are bloodshot red. I'm sure he thanked God that the hospital was not far away. He jumps out of the car, barely putting it in park.

"What's going on? What's wrong with Stella?" He's pushing past everyone.

"Nothing is wrong, Sir. She couldn't calm down after seeing your wife, so we gave her a sedative and are transporting her for further monitoring."

Rubbing his chest. "Oh, thank God. And my wife?"

"I'm sorry, Sir," the paramedic said shaking his head. "We were too late."

"Oh, god. No. No. No. No. No. No."

"Mr. Monrow, we need you to stay calm. Especially for Stella's sake. Ok?"

"Ok."

Off to the hospital I go.

Two days of people coming in and out.

Just let me sleep. I swear. I am good.

But because I am so stoic, they are *concerned*.

Chapter Twenty-Eight

The Funeral

One week goes by. Final funeral preparations are in order and so are my bag of tricks. Something in me said to grab all her valuable stuff and store it away while everyone was grieving. I grabbed all the jewelry, designer clothing, shoes, some electronics, and other junk. I'm not sure what to do with it yet, but I am sure it will be worth it.

The night before the funeral, I sneak into the funeral home. Technically, I don't really sneak or break in. I just stay after visitation hours. She's the last viewing. I tell David I'm staying with Zack and tell Zack I'm with David. It's no longer uncommon for me to turn off my phone, so there's that. No one bothers me either way.

I get to work. I find the obituaries and add an extra insert about David's infidelities.

Oh, shit. I bet you are wondering about the baby? Well, turns out it WASN'T David's! Holy shit!!

I nearly lost my shit when we found out.

The baby is being buried with his dear, old mother.

Awww, how cute.

Ok. Picture this. The baby is in a preemie outfit the same colors as Karen's. Karen is holding the baby as if they're sleeping.

Isn't that just fucking adorable?

I find the room where they're being kept. With a Sharpie, I write, in David's handwriting of course, "this is not David's baby" on the baby.

Oh, come on. Don't give me that look. I told you. She brought this on herself. NOT ME! I owe her for this life and all my stuff she destroyed. Including my innocence.

So, on the back of the extra insert is the DNA test. (I'm not even sure why he had suspicion, but I am totally glad he did.)

Turns out, Karen had a few secrets of her own. I was tasked with cleaning out her office. Ok, I volunteered. And if I had a teacup emoji, I would insert it here. Apparently, on the new job, Karen never told them she was married. She was getting it on good with this guy named Ian, the big boss of their division.

What they didn't say was how Ian is this rich, hot, black guy! She definitely finds the money. I find out this little morsel when Ian rounded the corner, and the secretary catches him and says Ian, how are you holding up?

You could have literally bought me for a quarter. I nearly stopped boxing up her belongings and just stared at him. Under different circumstances I would have tried to make him mine. But I love Zack so as quickly as that thought came into my mind, I pushed it out.

You should have seen my face!

So, now I get it! The little tint in DJ's skin would have been a reason to doubt. But, it is not *totally* out of the question as Karen's heritage has a bit of diversity in it.

*Oh. That's what they are calling him. DJ. For David Jr.,
Remember, appearances are everything.*

Besides, only one person knows. Well, two. Outside of
David and me, of course. And that's Dr. Conway and Dr.
Davis. Not even Lila knows. But she will now. I spare Ian
the humiliation because the poor soul didn't know. But I
really wanted to put his picture on there, too. I just say
the baby is DEFINITELY NOT WHITE on the excerpt, so
that can sink in.

I also plant pictures in the slideshow with the audio
from me catching David and Lila's conversation of "the
extra shot of morphine," his sexcapades, and anything
else that will be damning to him. And I loop it! I plaster
the flyers all over the inside of the casket with super
glue. (Good luck getting that off.) I also write WHORE on
Karen's forehead with the same Sharpie. In David's
handwriting, of course. I even sew on a real scarlet
letter A on her dress.

Let's be clear, Lila will not go unscathed. Her picture is
the largest and at the top of the insert with the caption;
IT ALL STARTED HERE.

I think this is enough damage. Plus, I'm tired. I sleep in the restroom and wait for the funeral home to open its doors before sneaking out. They won't know it's me. I investigated where the cameras are during the visitation. I also dressed in all black and covered my face and hands. I even took the liberty to find the office and erase what video I could. Seriously, as fancy as this place is, it should have a better security system. And don't have the passwords under the keyboard. #facepalm

I head home just in time. I climb the lattice and strip out of my clothes. I throw on my PJs and head out. David is crying something fierce and guess who's here. Take a wild guess. AS IF you had to. LI-fucking-LA!! I am sure I was definitely NOT missed for a second. I guess she's getting her opportunity once and for all. You know I didn't leave that suicide note out, right? As a matter of fact, a copy is on the insert. I make sure of that. It took some finessing, but I maneuvered it where the words don't cover up any of his dirty deeds. I had to make sure EVERYTHING was in view for ALL to see.

I walk past the room and stop. Is Lila wearing her lingerie?

Wow! Ok, I have to find out what is going on here.

I slide open the door. Sex is in the air for sure. Lila's crying, too.

"Are you guys ok?"

Lila speaks between tears. "Your dad is having a hard go at it. This hasn't been an easy time for him."

No, shit. And it's about to get worse. For you, too.

Also, does no one think it's odd that they're in the same bedroom where his wife just killed herself? Or that Lila is wearing the same dead wife's lingerie? Or sleeping in the same bed? Not to mention the fact that truly in my eyes, I am to think that Lila is "just a friend"?

I want to sing, *"But you say she's just a friend."*

Only a few of you will get that.

"Dad?" He reaches his hand for me. Eh. I oblige.

"Stella. How are you? I know these past few years hasn't been the best to you, either."

"I'm ok, Dad. Really, I am."

"You've always been a trooper. I'm sorry I wasn't there for you more. I recognize that now."

Too late, buddy.

"Oh, it's ok. I think I will survive." I glance at the table clock. "It's getting late. We better start getting ready. The limo will be here shortly."

We skip breakfast, and I am starving. I text Zack to bring me something to snack on. He brings me a sausage sandwich. It's either really good, or I'm very hungry. Or both. He arrives at the funeral home at the same time as the limo. Mom and Jonathan are there. I told her she didn't *have* to be here, but somehow, I think she is getting a really sick thrill from it and I like it.

Something else strikes me. When Lila gets out of the car, Mom's face changes. I think she puts it together. But Jonathan is hot and built, whereas David is now scrawny looking and decrepit.

It's not gloomy outside, and that's surprising. The sun is shining, and it feels good on my skin. I'm happy that Zack is here. Kelsi and Richard show up, too. We all sit together. I purposely hide the programs so they'll be passed out during the service. It takes a minute, but everyone is seated, and they find the programs and began passing them out along with… da da da DA!! THE SLIDESHOW. They open the casket and the "Oh My God's" start. Those in the back don't get to see it all. BUT EVERYONE gets a program!

HAAAAAAAAAAAAA!!

Even my mother is like, "This isn't right!"

Time to play shocked. I snatch the program out of Zack's hand.

I deserve an Oscar.

"Who did this?! Why would you ruin my dad's name?! What no-class son of a bitch did *THIS*?! This is a FUNERAL for God's sake!" I drop to the floor, and I don't even know where the tears come from! Zack and

Richard rush to pick me up. Kelsi looks like she's about to vomit.

Dad literally pisses himself and Lila... well, let's just say that is the quickest exit I have ever seen. And people are watching the video! One asshole goes live recording it. It is priceless!

Chapter Twenty-Nine

Play the Role

The next few weeks, I stay mostly at Mom's. Kind of like how it should have been. Life was a complete hell for David. All his patients leave in a heartbeat. The hospital lets him go. The police are crawling everywhere. No skank will return his call. Not even Lila.

He does get the insurance money. They can't stop that. I make sure I know where every drop of his money goes. (Mostly to the lawyers.) Though, I keep track of what's left.

The police are investigating David, as he is now a suspect in Karen's death.

I might have helped in that. I might have placed the suicide note in the drawer where they could find it. I might have sent an anonymous note to the police to treat it as a murder case, as he might have coerced her into taking the pills. I might have spilled about those two fights. And I might have said that he was on cocaine.

Plus, the coroner's first preliminary toxicology report prompts them to do a thorough investigation (although it was late).

The police are absolutely certain that his motive was the insurance money, as they were heavily in debt.

To me, that's a bonus. When I overhear Mom talking to the neighbor one day, it takes everything in my body not to fall out laughing. My plan succeeded more than I expected. Mom comes in and begins to prepare dinner.

There is an unusual knock on the door. Mom looks at the camera to see who it is.

She walks to the window for a better view. As she looks out the window, there is an awkward look on her face. I creep closer to the top of the stairs to listen.

"Yes, detective. I know."

"Do you think she will be able to talk to us for a few minutes? With your permission, of course."

"Yes. I don't see why not. Stella!"

I quickly run back to my room and call out. "Yes, Ma'am?"

"Come here, honey. I have some people that need to speak with you."

"Yes, Ma'am." I walk to the steps coolly and descend them calmly, as not to raise any suspicion.

"Hi, Stella. I'm Detective Wells." She extends her hand and I shake it. "And this is Detective Finley."

"Hello."

"Can I ask you some questions about your dad?"

My god, she is hot! A detective? More like a model to me.

Mom lets them in, and we sit on the living room couch. Detective Wells is this beautiful, black woman who is dressed more for the runway than fighting crime. She is gorgeous. Her skin is like a sun-kissed goddess. Her hair is curly and pulled up neatly in a bun. I swear. I wouldn't leave Zack alone with her.

Detective Finley, on the other hand, is dressed like he just woke up, showered, and got dressed. If he had taken five more minutes on his grooming, they would be the perfect couple. He's still good-looking. It's something about the gun on his side that makes me want to show him how grown up I am.

"Sure. Ok."

"Was your dad acting strangely at all?" We sit on the couch. Finley paces the floor looking at pictures. Maybe he's taking mental notes.

"Um. No. Not to my knowledge."

"Did you ever hear them arguing?"

"A couple of times about his cheating, but I know he loved Mom."

"I'm confused." She raises an eyebrow. I am half tempted to kiss her on the lips.

"I mean my stepmom."

"I'm her biological mother. We're both named Karen. She was just, *younger.*"

Mom, let it be known!

"Oh."

"She insisted that I call her 'mom' to make the family a little more at ease and in unison. She wasn't that good at the mom thing, but I was pretty much brainwashed to do so to make her happy."

"How did you feel about that?"

"At first, I didn't like it. But I'm a kid. What kid do you know that wants to see their parents split? And the new person tries to replace what is already there? Besides, I don't like causing trouble, so I went along. To get along."

"Yeah. I guess you're right. So, did your dad have money troubles?"

"What do you mean? He's a doctor."

"What were the bills like? Did he do a lot of spending?"

"Uh, no. Not that I know of. Except during the holidays. I know this last Christmas he spent way more than usual but he didn't complain. He said once that he regretted buying the house because it was so expensive. But before that? No. She handled everything. He just gave her the money."

"Oh. I see. Ok. Well, thank you, Stella. One other question. Did you tell your mother that she hit you?"

"No, she didn't!" (Too high-pitched for my liking.) "Where did you hear that?"

My voice goes up three octaves. I'm actually in shock and caught off guard by that one. Hell, I forgot about it, honestly.

Detective Finley raises a furrowed brow this time. "According to the medical report at the urgent care," He flips through his notes. "You received seven stitches, and you begged them not to contact the authorities according to the nurse."

Oh shit! I glance over at Mom, and she is fuming!

Damn! Think!

"We–well. She thought I had done something to her cat. But I mean, it wasn't that serious. Really. It wasn't. Besides, my mom had enough to deal with. Dad said it was best that we didn't tell anyone."

Cue waterworks.

"Mom. I'm so sorry. I didn't want to get anyone in trouble. *I* didn't want to get in trouble."

"Thank you, Stella." Detective Wells just calms the air.

"Ok. My dad's not in trouble, is he?"

"I don't know, darling." The detectives leave, and inside, I'm smiling from ear to ear.

Chapter Thirty

David's in Trouble

I find that the more trouble David is in, the more I relish it. I find so much pleasure in knowing that he is hurting. Even more than Mom did when he left her.

Secretly, I know Mom delights in it, too. To a degree.

Then, a sickening feeling comes over me. *What if I had planned this all too well? What if they think my mom convinced me to do it?*

I have to shake this off and remain calm. It is very important for me to stay with Mom.

Time passes, and David is on trial for murder. I won't bore you with those details. Typical trial. Typical scandal.

The evidence is stacked up against him. And no one is the wiser. David lost his license and many court dates later, he lost his freedom, too. David is sentenced to life in prison.

Lila skips town as fast as she can. The detectives are looking for her, but part of the plea deal was that they wouldn't pursue her any further and leave her be. Last I heard, she's doing quite well for herself. She found someone that wanted to marry her and had a baby right away.

The trial only takes nearly a year and a half. The whole time, David is in jail. He tried reaching out to Lila, probably to help him make bail, but she never contacted him back. I understand why. I mean, did he really expect her to be there even if she wasn't being pursued? Silly rabbit.

They tell me I don't have to testify, but I want to. Of course, I don't tell him that. I tell him I want to testify on his behalf, but I'm under oath and can't lie. He buys it. Mom only shows up a few times. She can't bear to hear all of the infidelities or stomach how he looks.

It's crazy. I make sure I'm there to play my part. Through it all, Kelsi and Zack stay by my side. I even make sure to add a sniffle every now and again. I want it to be over so I can get on with my life.

Karen's family came for everything they could after the trial began. Well, I wasn't about to let that happen. Like I said earlier. Something told me to stash her stuff.

They wanted the insurance money. They try suing him, but that's postponed because of the trial. If it was a family heirloom I gave it to them. They even ask for stuff David bought her. I tell them that we tossed it out. I also found out that he never put her name on anything, so Mom inherits it all.

Sweet, sweet justice.

When Karen's family finally gives up their gold-digging ways, Mom and I start selling everything. David has no chance for parole so why not capitalize on it? We sell the house and split it 50/50. She gives me control of my trust fund and college fund — anything that isn't bolted to the house…sold. We sell every last bit of his belongings too.

Why not?

What we don't or can't sell, we donate.

Between it all, school is fabulous. Zack stays true to me at college. Occasionally, I go visit him and we spend the weekends together. I'm now in my senior year, and I still visit David from time to time. I guess I have to. Honestly, I want to. I need to see how sick he is.

Poor David. See what your infidelity cost you?

Each day, my hatred for him grows. First, for him splitting up the family the way he did. Second, for taking me away from my mom. (He KNEW nothing was wrong with her and they used a ruse to get full custody.) And finally, for making me do all of this to get rid of Karen.

Then, no hope of him getting back with Mom when she pleaded with him not to leave. Including saying that he could have her as a mistress. It wasn't fair that Mom had or tried to plea with him and losing a part of herself.

All I wanted was my family back, and he couldn't see that. He couldn't see that I needed to be whole. To feel what I had from birth.

Now, here I am without a father. Thankfully, Jonathan fills in just fine.

Chapter Thirty-One

The Start of a Better Life

Senior year is going without a hitch. Mom and Jonathan have decided to get married. I call him "Father" and "Dad." Truthfully, he is way better at it. But for you to understand, I will continue to call him Jonathan.

It isn't long before Mom and Jonathan have their beautiful wedding. He takes her to Tahiti for their honeymoon. She comes back so sun-kissed and beautiful. I have never seen her look so happy, especially in recent years. She looks like her old self. Jonathan is so good for her and to her.

Zack and I talk about how our relationship will be for both of us.

I stop visiting David in prison by my sophomore year in college. The sight of him disgusts me. The same overwhelming disgust that I felt for Karen.

What made it worse was that he never stopped talking about her. What went wrong, how much he really loved her, and how he really messed up.

Even after all of this!

I sit there seething until I slam my fists on the table. The officer looks at us but ignores the disruption.

Finally, I blow up and tell him the truth.

"You know what?" I say, barely in a whisper and through clenched teeth so no one could hear me. "I killed her. I took pleasure in every moment of killing her. I even took joy from when they fingered you for the crime. You are a sick, stupid, weak, and poor excuse for a man. That woman saw what we had, and she wanted it. You let her in, and she hurt my mother. Hell, she cheated on you. It was never about love with her. It was about money and appearance. Yes, I *killed* her! I gave her the pills. I wrote the note. I did it. I killed BOTH cats. I turned you in. *I* testified *AGAINST* you! And the funeral..." I let my mouth fall open. "You deserve even worse than this. If I had my way, I would kill you, too!

You ruined our family. Most importantly, you ruined me."

It's obvious that my words sting like venom.

"Stella. I did no such thing!"

It turns into a screaming match.

"Yes, you did! Yes, you did! You let her seduce you. You let her subtly plant things into your head about Mom. You let her take me away from Mom! I would have been fine, but you let her convince YOU that Mom was unfit. She wasn't! She took really good care of me! She was there for every school function, and they loved her! And you took that away from me!"

And for the second time in my life, actual, real tears flow from my eyes.

"How selfish of you to not think of your child and just of your own needs!" I cry. "I HATE YOU! Don't ever worry about me ever coming to see you again!"

I storm out as officers come to see what the ruckus is all about. I push past one and keep moving as if I hadn't just bumped him. He stands in disbelief and yet, has to chuckle.

David stands, calling after me. "Stella! Stella! Stella! What do you mean you killed her?"

The officers grabs him and escorts him towards his cell.

"Wait! Wait! She knows something regarding my wife's death. Wait. Stop her! She said she killed my wife!"

"Sir, please calm down."

"No, wait. She's ruined my life!"

"Not from what we heard."

Epilogue

I don't see David again after that last visit in the prison.

I don't regret that decision to do everything I did and to confess it to him.

They never further investigate what David told them I said.

In fact, it drives him insane.

No one visits him, not even his own parents. When they die two years later, three months apart, no one bats an eye about him not being there.

To be certain, I send a request that they deny him the opportunity to attend their funerals. I was nice enough, however, to mail him the obituaries.

At least he would have that, right?

But I never take a call from him or visit him. No one does. Frankly, because of all the scandal, I don't blame them.

Six months later, I receive word that David committed suicide.

I don't cry. In fact, I don't feel anything. I finally have closure.

Life is good. Really good.

I start attending service regularly with my mom. I change a lot. I leave that part of my life behind. It takes a lot of counseling. Of course, I would never confess what I did to another person. That is between me and God and I will take it to my grave.

I even get baptized.

All of us do. Me, Mom, Zack, Kelsi, and Richard. That day is a true family affair.

Zack and I finally get married. He and Richard graduate. Kelsi and I are doing great. We are working on opening our business together while attending school. Zack is a full-time Architect, and Richard is working on his Doctorate.

I never tell anyone else what I did and how I did it. I bury it. I get rid of everything in the old fashion way by throwing things away in separate bins in separate neighborhoods. Destroying all files, photos, and videos.

I practically erase all traces of evidence that it ever happened, except in my memory.

I want a good life, and by God, I am going to have it.

That is my revenge.

About the Author

Patricia Brothers was born and raised in St. Louis, Missouri. She is a mother of two. She is currently working on her degree in Organizational Leadership with an emphasis in Psychology. In her high school days, writing and acting were some of her favorite past times. She has been the lead actress in two plays and has held multiple supporting roles. Being an author has always been her dream. While she has held many positions in the corporate world, she never let go of that dream.

Follow the author on social media:

Facebook: Patricia Brothers (Author)

Instagram and Twitter: @TriciaBwriting

Email: TriciaBWriting@gmail.com

Black Butterfly Books

Is an imprint of

The Butterfly Typeface Publishing.

Books to intelligently entertain the discriminating reader!

Contact us for all your

publishing & writing needs!